# TO THE RESCUE!

"Mrs. Reg is gone for the week," Max said. "She had to go visit a sick friend who called her yesterday afternoon. She won't be back until Friday, and there are a zillion and one things she left me to do. This is a very busy week. . . . I don't know how I'll ever—"

The phone rang. Max picked it up. He barely said a word, but as soon as he hung up, he dashed back out the door.

"This is our chance, girls," Stevie said. "It gives us a four-day head start on finishing what we started last night. We're going to run Pine Hollow for Max this week while Mrs. Reg is gone. It's the perfect opportunity for the three of us to be everywhere, look everywhere, do everything. If that pin is here, anywhere, we're going to find it."

"And if we don't?" Carole asked.

Stevie shrugged. "Well, then, we will have spent the week earning dozens and dozens of brownie points. How could Max and Mrs. Reg want to kill us when we're indispensable. . . ."

*With special thanks to the Usual Suspects: Nicole and Marilyn. B.B.H.*
*(Ghost Rider)*

Random House Australia Pty Ltd
20 Alfred Street, Milsons Point NSW 2061
http://www.randomhouse.com.au

Sydney New York Toronto
London Auckland Johannesburg
and agencies throughout the world

'Horse Trouble' and 'Ghost Rider' first published in the United States
in 1992 by Bantam Skylark Books,
a division of Random House Inc.
Copyright © 1992 by Bonnie Bryant Hiller.
'The Saddle Club' is a registered trademark of Bonnie Bryant Hiller

Random House Australia Edition 2002

National Library of Australia
Cataloguing-in-Publication Data

Bryant, Bonnie.
Horse trouble & ghost rider.

ISBN 1 74051 794 6.

1. Horses – Juvenile fiction. 2. Riding clubs – Juvenile fiction. I.
Bryant, Bonnie. Ghost Rider. II. Title. (Series : Byrant, Bonnie.
Saddle Club).

813.54

Cover photograph by Dennis Wisken/Greg Noakes courtesy Crawfords
Australia.
Cover design by Jobi Murphy.
Printed by Griffin Press Pty Ltd, Adelaide.

# the Saddle Club

# Horse Trouble +
# Ghost Rider

Bonnie Bryant

RANDOM HOUSE AUSTRALIA

LISA ATWOOD FELT great. It was a Monday afternoon, and she'd managed to spend almost every minute of the day at Pine Hollow Stable. She'd spent one hour of that time in a jump class and two hours on a trail ride with her Pony Club, Horse Wise. Summer was her favorite time of year because it meant she could spend a lot of time with horses.

It also meant she could spend a lot of time with friends. Her two best friends, Stevie Lake and Carole Hanson, loved horses just as much as she did. The three of them were all so wild about horses that they had formed their own group, The Saddle Club. There were only two requirements for membership. The first was that the members had to be horse crazy. The second was that they had to be willing to help one another out, no matter what the problem was. When one of the girls got into trouble, two friends were always there to help get her out. Lisa liked that, although she wasn't usually the one who got into trouble.

Even the fact that the girls had all been given chores to do around the stable after class didn't dispel Lisa's happy mood. She knew it was one of the ways Max Regnery, Pine Hollow's owner and chief instructor, kept his expenses down: All the riders pitched in to take care of the animals. Lisa thought it was one of the best things about riding at Pine Hollow. Although she wasn't absolutely wild about mucking out stables, she knew that loving horses meant taking care of them, not just riding them. She was glad to do her part.

Mrs. Reg, Max's mother, was the stable manager. All the young riders adored her, though they weren't too crazy about her habit of assigning chores. If Mrs. Reg saw two girls chatting, she was sure to give them a job while they chatted. Since girls often liked to chat—most especially Stevie, Lisa, and Carole—they often found themselves doing chores like measuring and mixing grains for feed or soaping saddles. This afternoon Mrs. Reg had them moving and checking bales of hay for mold and mildew. It was an important job because moldy hay could make horses sick, but it was difficult and sweaty work on a summer day. The good thing about it now was that it was done, and Lisa was ready to report that fact to Mrs. Reg.

She stepped into Mrs. Reg's office. Mrs. Reg was on the phone, with a serious look on her face. Lisa knew better than to interrupt. Also, from the look on Mrs. Reg's face, she doubted that she *could* interrupt. Mrs. Reg was definitely not aware of her presence. She stepped back out of the office until Mrs. Reg hung up, trying hard not to listen. When she heard the phone put back in its cradle, she reentered. Mrs. Reg looked right up at her. Lisa smiled broadly and saluted.

"The hay-bale task force has completed its inspection, ma'am," she joked. "I'm pleased to report that all of the hay appears to be fresh and mold free!"

Normally Mrs. Reg would like that kind of joking. This time she didn't seem to get it. "Are you sure?" she asked.

Lisa dropped her saluting arm and her pretense. "Of course I'm sure," she said. "We looked over all the bales and everything's fine. No sign of anything amiss. You can trust us, you know."

Mrs. Reg smiled at her then. "I'm sorry, Lisa. I know you know what you're doing. I think I'm sort of distracted. . . ."

Lisa realized it had to be the phone call. Mrs. Reg seemed a little embarrassed, but didn't want to talk about it. That made Lisa feel a little embarrassed, too. She wanted to say something, but she wasn't sure what. Her eyes went to Mrs. Reg's desk, where there was something shining in the afternoon sunlight, and she was very surprised by what she saw.

"What's that?" she asked, looking at a beautiful gold pin.

Mrs. Reg smiled again. "Pretty, isn't it? Go ahead, pick it up."

Lisa did. The pin was of a horse, galloping full out, its tail sailing dramatically behind. It was gold with a brush finish that made the horse seem silky and sleek. And the horse's eye was a diamond that sparkled brightly even in the dim indoor light of Mrs. Reg's office.

"It's not just pretty," Lisa said. "It's *beautiful.*"

"Max gave it to me," Mrs. Reg said. "My Max, I mean." Lisa knew that meant her husband, who had died long ago, not her son, who now ran the stable. "It would be our fortieth wedding anniversary this week. It was his wedding present for me."

Lisa held the pin carefully, turning it, admiring the art and the artistry. She'd seen lots of horse jewelry. The Saddle Club even had its own pin, and she always thought that was pretty, too. But she'd never seen anything as beautiful as this.

"Have Stevie and Carole seen it?" she asked.

"I doubt it," Mrs. Reg said. "I don't usually wear it around here."

Lisa could understand why. A stable was no place for valuables—except horses, of course. "Can I show it to them?"

"Sure," Mrs. Reg said. "I have to talk with Max—*your* Max—about something now. If I'm not here when you bring it back, just put it in my center drawer, okay?"

"Okay, thanks," Lisa said, glad that Mrs. Reg knew she could trust her. That was one advantage to being reliable. People trusted you when it really mattered.

Holding the pin carefully, but not too tightly, she left Mrs. Reg's office and returned to the locker area, where her friends were already changing into their street clothes. They'd made a plan to have a Saddle Club meeting at their favorite hangout, an ice-cream parlor called TD's, right after class. Stevie had said she thought it was a really good idea because she had heard her mother was serving calves' liver for dinner, and she wanted to ruin her appetite.

5

Stevie was like that. She was fun-loving and mischievous. Carole, on the other hand, was the most serious horsewoman of the three of them. She had been riding since she was a very little girl and had long since decided that when she grew up, she would work with horses. All that remained was to decide exactly how she would work with them—whether she'd be a rider, trainer, breeder, veterinarian, instructor, or all of them. When the subject was horses, Carole was all business. On any other subject, she could sometimes be a little flaky.

Lisa was the newest rider of the three, but she'd learned fast, and Max already said she was very good. She was earnest, logical, and methodical about everything she did. She was also a straight-A student and rarely got into trouble, unless dragged there by Stevie.

It always amazed Lisa and her friends how different the three of them were and how much they liked one another in spite of—or perhaps because of—their differences. Of course they had being horse crazy in common, and another thing they shared was an intense dislike of one Veronica diAngelo—a member of their riding class. Veronica was a snooty rich girl who mistakenly believed that because she was rich, she was better than everybody else. The Saddle Club girls thought that she was worse than everybody else, and it had nothing whatsoever to do with her money. It was her basic rotten personality. Lisa wasn't particularly pleased to see that Veronica was in the locker area when she entered to show her friends Mrs. Reg's pin. She held it so that Veronica couldn't see it and sashayed past the girl to her friends. Veronica didn't seem to notice. She was too busy studying her reflection in her compact to see anything but herself. For once Lisa was glad for Veronica's incredible vanity.

"Look at this pin of Mrs. Reg's," Lisa said, holding it out to show her friends.

"Oh, the diamond is so perfect!" Stevie said. "Wouldn't it be wonderful if we could have a pin like that for The Saddle Club?"

Lisa looked at the very special silver horse-head pin on her shirt. She liked Mrs. Reg's pin, but she wouldn't trade her Saddle Club pin for anything. "I don't know . . . ," she began.

"The conformation!" Carole said. Stevie and Lisa stifled giggles. It was just like Carole to look at the characteristics of the horse rather than just the beauty of the jewelry. "And with a head like that, it's got to be an Arabian."

Lisa and Stevie looked again, seeing the pin anew. Of course, Carole was right. The horse was definitely an Arabian—sleek and beautiful.

"What are you looking at?" Veronica asked, suddenly interested. Veronica's own horse was a purebred Arabian mare named Garnet.

Lisa, Stevie, and Carole looked at one another. All had the same thought. Veronica was looking for a way to put them all down. They just *had* to make it impossible for her to do. There was a light in Stevie's eyes.

"Oh, it's just this pin of mine," she said casually, holding it out to Veronica, who took it from her. "Kind of pretty, isn't it?"

Since that was such an obvious understatement, it was enough to silence Veronica for a few seconds while Stevie collected her thoughts. "My brother Chad gave it to me last Christmas," she went on. "It's a nice piece of costume jewelry, don't you think?"

If there was one thing Veronica thought she knew a lot about, it was real jewelry. Telling her that this was fake made it impossible for her to insult the jewelry or Stevie any further. All Veronica could do now was stare at the beautiful pin in her hand, unable to think of anything cutting to say beyond, "Nice, for a fake," which she muttered reluctantly. Stevie beamed proudly.

And then the ruckus began. At first there was just a minor skittering sound, then an unmistakable squeak.

It was followed by a small flash of gray moving quickly across the locker-area floor. That, in turn, was followed by a much larger flash of black and white named Man o' War. The gray was a mouse; the black and white was a cat in hot pursuit.

It was a fact of life that stables have mice. That's why most stables also have cats to keep down the mouse population and Man o' War was just doing his job. The girls, however, and most especially Veronica, wished he were doing it somewhere else.

Veronica leapt up onto the bench and began screaming. The mouse, now even more frightened, ran out from under the bench and stood in the middle of the floor, frozen in terror. It was the opportunity Man o' War had been waiting for. He pounced. That made the mouse move. Fast. That made Veronica scream. That made the cat howl. The mouse fled toward the horse stalls. The cat followed—*very* fast.

That might have been the end of it except that the mouse chose to look for an escape route in the stall of one of the stable's newest horses, an injured and retired racer by the name of Prancer. Lisa knew that most horses have at least one thing that scares them. In the wild such fears protect horses. They know what they have to flee from, and once they know, there's almost nothing that can be done to alleviate that fear.

In Prancer's case, the fear was cats. The moment she spotted Man o' War climbing up and over the doorway to her stall, she began fussing. She whinnied and cried out.

From the sound of the horse's cry, Carole recognized exactly what was happening and that it could be big trouble. Prancer was still recovering from a fracture in her foot that had cost her her career as a racehorse and might well cost her her life if it didn't heal well. A frightened horse could get into awful trouble. She needed to be calmed right away.

"Come on!" she said to her friends. She didn't have to say it twice.

The three girls ran to the stalls and found that the cat had the mouse cornered in the stall. The mouse was stunned by fear; the cat knew he had the upper hand and wasn't about to move. Prancer jumped and kicked, preparing to rear.

Without even thinking about it, Carole and Stevie each grabbed a lead rope. If they could just get the ropes clipped to the horse's halter, they'd have a chance to control her. But there was no way they could go into the stall when she was so upset. Sending one of the three of them off to the hospital wasn't a very good idea.

Stevie and Carole climbed up on the stall door and

tried to reach for the halter. While they did that, Lisa did what she thought was the most logical thing. She took a broom and went into the stall next to Prancer's. That housed a sweet-natured pinto named Patch, who watched all the events going on around him with only mild curiosity. Lisa hiked herself up onto the top of the divider separating the two stalls and reached down with the broom. She could just barely touch the floor of the stall, but that was all she needed. She stretched as far as she could and put the broom right next to the mouse.

This mouse was no fool. Just as Lisa had hoped, he understood that he was in dire straits and immediately scootched into the safety of the broom bristles, holding on for dear life. As soon as Lisa thought she might have the mouse, she lifted the broom back over the divider, left Patch's stall as fast as possible, and took her hostage to the door of the stable, where she shook the broom. A stunned mouse fell out of the bristles. Within half a second he righted himself, looked around, and headed for the tall grass, where Lisa was sure his family was waiting for him. He'd have quite a story to tell them. She paused briefly to wonder how he would explain the miracle of the broom.

When Lisa got back to the stall, however, she found that only half the problem had been solved. The mouse was gone, but Man o' War was still standing in the stall and Prancer was still scared.

"Calm down, girl," Carole was saying. Horses liked to have people talk to them. Prancer particularly liked it when Carole talked to her. The horse seemed to adore Carole, and it was obviously mutual. "Everything's going to be fine. We'll just get that cat out, and you don't have anything to worry about. Poor cat's just as scared as you are."

Lisa looked at the cat. He didn't appear scared, just confused. He couldn't figure out where his dinner had gone!

"Try the broom trick again," Stevie suggested, still trying unsuccessfully to reach for Prancer's halter. For a second Lisa tried to figure out if the cat could possibly hold onto the broom's bristles as the mouse had, but then she realized that wasn't what Stevie meant. She reentered Patch's stall, remounted the divider, and re-reached over with the broom.

The cat saw it coming and he didn't like what he saw. Dodging with his head, he spun a full one hundred eighty degrees and dashed up and out of the stall as fast as he'd dashed into it. Then there was quiet. Prancer looked around, trying to assure herself that the cat was actually gone. Finally the horse relaxed as suddenly as she'd shied. She reached for her hay feeder, grabbed a few strands of sweet hay, and munched. Then she looked up at the three girls still perched on the walls and door of her stall. A quizzical looked crossed the horse's face as if to wonder what on earth all the fuss was about. The girls had been dismissed and they knew it.

"What teamwork!" Lisa said.

"This calls for a celebration," Stevie agreed.

"TD's?" Carole suggested.

It was just what they had in mind.

It DIDN'T TAKE long before Lisa realized something was wrong. The three girls sat at their favorite booth at TD's and talked about what had happened with Prancer, Man o' War, and the mouse.

"You should have seen the look on that mouse's face when I set him free in the paddock!" Lisa said gleefully. "I mean, his eyes were shining like, like— like . . ." She could see the bright shine in the little creature's eyes, glistening in the outdoor sunlight nearly sparkling. " . . . oh, no."

"Like what?" Stevie asked.

"Diamonds," Lisa said, a look of horror crossing her face. She didn't have to say it again or explain. The moment she uttered the word, her friends knew exactly what she'd just remembered.

"Let's go," Carole said. The girls left TD's in a shot, leaving behind a confused waitress.

"We'll be right back!" Carole called.

"Right after we get out of prison!" Stevie added.

The restaurant door slammed behind them. They didn't even hear it, they were running so fast.

TD's was just a short distance from Pine Hollow. The girls often walked it after class, and it usually took them about ten minutes. This time they covered the distance in less than five minutes—at a run.

"It's got to be in the locker area!" Lisa said breathlessly over her shoulder.

"Yeah," Carole agreed. "That's where it was when we had to save Prancer."

"We'll find it. Don't worry," Stevie said. They all liked the sound of those words. They just hoped they were true.

There was nobody in the locker area when they got there. That wasn't surprising. All the young riders—the only ones who used this room, were long gone. Nobody would be back there until tomorrow. Lisa dropped to her hands and knees to look at the floor. Stevie looked at every surface in the place—tables, benches, and shelves. Carole focused on the tops of the lockers, and when they proved clean (not of dust, just of pins), she began looking in the lockers.

There wasn't a sign of the pin.

The locker area was small, and it didn't take the girls long to be absolutely sure that the pin wasn't there. To be definitely, positively, totally sure, they each switched levels and repeated the search. Then the three of them worked together to move the lockers away from the wall just to see if the pin might have slipped behind them. They found a riding crop there. They didn't find a gold pin with a diamond in it.

"Veronica," Lisa said. "She was the one who was holding it when the cat and the mouse came through. Maybe she took it."

"Veronica would never take a piece of jewelry she thought wasn't real," Stevie said.

"Maybe so, but I think I'd better call her to see if she remembers what happened," Lisa said. Stevie and Carole agreed that was a good idea, and Lisa went to use the phone in Mrs. Reg's office. Normally riders were expected to use the pay phone, but in the case of an emergency, they were allowed to use the stable phone. Lisa thought this qualified as an emergency.

Mrs. Reg's office was empty and dark. When she turned on the light and sat to use the phone, she was struck by the fact that the desk, which had been in its usual state of disorganization when she'd last been in there just over an hour earlier, was now neat as a—she didn't even want to *think* the word—pin. Perhaps Mrs. Reg was turning over a new leaf, Lisa mused quickly as she picked up the phone. Then she cringed as she thought of the more likely answer. Mrs. Reg had straightened everything up looking for her pin. Lisa hated the idea of causing anybody such trouble. She dialed Veronica's number.

Veronica answered the phone herself, which was not surprising since it was her own private telephone line. Lisa explained that the girls had been looking for the horse pin and wondered if Veronica knew what had happened to it.

There was quite a pause. "Pin, pin," Veronica said, repeating the word to remind herself what Lisa was talking about. "Oh, that old pin that Stevie's brother gave her?" At least she remembered it. "I don't know," Veronica went on. "I think I threw the darn thing at the cat. Is that all you want to know?"

It was. Lisa told her so and hung up, now more worried than ever.

"Lisa, is that you?" It was Max. He was surprised to find Lisa in his mother's office.

"I just had to make a call," Lisa said quickly. "I'm sorry, but I didn't have change."

"No problem," Max said. "Just don't tell the whole world I didn't make a fuss, okay?" He grinned at her. Max was really a wonderful person. That made it particularly hard on Lisa, knowing she was lying to him. "Isn't it time for you to get home now?" Max asked. "We want you rested and well for tomorrow's jump class. You're doing very well, you know. I'm awfully flattered. You should be, too."

"Thanks, Max," she said, and in spite of the fact that her mind wasn't on her riding, she was very pleased by his words. Max wasn't usually very free with compliments. "I'm on my way now," she said. "Stevie and Carole are waiting for me. Good night."

She couldn't leave fast enough. There was no point in staying at Pine Hollow. There was nothing there for them. They'd made absolutely sure of that.

The three girls left Pine Hollow for the second time that afternoon. Stevie and Lisa lived near one another. Carole was going home with Stevie because her father was picking her up at Stevie's house instead of at the stable, since he wouldn't be able to get off work for another hour. They didn't talk much as they walked. Stevie had just one question.

"Was Veronica lying?"

Lisa mentally ran through the brief phone conversation again. She would have liked to say she thought

Veronica was lying, but the fact was she was just about certain she wasn't. For one thing, Veronica had a real disdain for fake jewelry. She had a real disdain for anything that didn't cost a lot of money. For another thing, in spite of all the awful things Lisa could say about her—and there were a lot of them—Veronica wasn't a thief.

"No," Lisa said finally. "She really believed the thing was a fake, and she would never be interested in something that wasn't real. Veronica is not the culprit. Trouble is, I don't know who is. I guess that means it's me." Without another word, she split off from Carole and Stevie and headed for her house.

"See you tomorrow," Stevie called after her, trying to sound cheerful. Lisa just grunted in response.

"Poor Lisa," Stevie said. "She just feels awful. I guess I do, too."

"I'm getting a feeling," Stevie said.

"What kind of feeling?" Carole asked.

"I'm getting a feeling that our friend needs our help," Stevie said.

"Yes, it's definitely a Saddle Club project," Carole agreed. "All we have to do is figure out what happened to the pin, find it, and get it back to Mrs. Reg before she notices that it's gone."

"I have a new motto for The Saddle Club," Stevie

said. "'The difficult we do immediately; the impossible takes a little longer.'"

One of the few things Stevie's friends loved most about her was her ability to find something to laugh about in the darkest moments.

"But how *much* longer?" Carole asked. This time she couldn't laugh.

THE NEXT MORNING Lisa was feeling no better about the awful situation than she had the night before.

"Why hasn't Mrs. Reg called?" Lisa asked herself. She stood in front of the mirror in her bathroom, combing her hair and getting ready for the disaster that this day was sure to be. She'd been in front of the mirror, practicing explanations for more than half an hour. None of them seemed adequate, even when paired with her most sincere apologies. And every time she closed her eyes, she saw an image of the pin, gold glinting in the sun, diamond eye sparkling brightly. Now it was gone.

Then she answered her own question. The reason Mrs. Reg hadn't called was that she trusted Lisa. She knew Lisa would never do anything careless with her valuable pin, and she knew that whatever reason Lisa had for not putting it in her drawer last night, as she'd promised, was a good one, and Lisa would be there with the pin in the morning.

Only she wouldn't be. Mrs. Reg was wrong this time. Lisa was not trustworthy. She'd gotten so interested in playing a joke on Veronica and then on chasing a cat and a mouse that she'd forgotten all about a golden horse. She didn't deserve Mrs. Reg's trust, and she knew she would never have it again.

She met Stevie and Carole outside Pine Hollow. Without a word, the three girls entered together and walked straight to Mrs. Reg's office. If they had to face the music, they wanted to get it over with and they wanted to do it together.

Mrs. Reg's office was still dark. The desk was still as neat as a pin. There was nobody there.

"What are you looking for?" Max asked. There was a slight edge to his voice.

"Where's Mrs. Reg?" Lisa asked.

"She's gone for the week," he said. "She had to go visit a sick friend who called her yesterday afternoon. She won't be back until Friday, and there are a zillion and one things she left me to do. This is a very busy week—I'm training a new horse for one of my show riders who expects a perfect mount by Friday—and now I have to manage the stable as well. Never mind that there's a new class beginning and I don't know what else. Mother said something about a list of things that have to get done. I don't know how I'll ever—"

The phone rang. Max picked it up. He barely said a word, but as soon as he hung up, he dashed back out the door.

"This is our chance, girls," Stevie said.

"Chance?" Lisa echoed. "What do you mean? You think this gives us a four-day head start on running out of the country?"

"No," Stevie said. "It gives us a four-day head start on finishing what we started last night. We're going to run Pine Hollow for Max this week while Mrs. Reg is gone. Don't you see? It's going to be the perfect opportunity for the three of us to be everywhere, look everywhere, do everything. If that pin is here, anywhere, we're going to find it."

"And if we don't?" Carole asked.

Stevie shrugged. "Well, then, we will have spent the week earning dozens and dozens of brownie points. How could Max and Mrs. Reg want to kill us when we're indispensable?"

Lisa and Carole considered the situation. Stevie's suggestion had some merit. It was also a whole lot better than the explanations and apologies that Lisa had been practicing, and it had the benefit of possibly accomplishing what appeared to be the impossible—finding the pin.

"It's worth trying," Lisa said.

Carole thought so, too. She thought about how hard the week would be as they tried to keep up a full schedule of classes and chores, plus manage the stable *and* find the pin. They would certainly be exhausted by the time Friday rolled around. She had an idea.

"Then, after it's all over" (and we've been banished from Pine Hollow for life, she thought, but did not say), "why don't you plan to come to my house on Friday for a dinner and a sleepover? I promised Dad I'd cook for him, and I want to try a new recipe I saw for vegetable lasagna—"

"I'll make Rice Krispie treats," Stevie suggested. It was one thing she was really good at cooking.

"I think we should plan for crow on the menu," Lisa said glumly.

"No way," Stevie said. "I think Carole's right. We should be looking on the bright side of things. We're going to do a wonderful job of managing the stable *and* we're going to find the pin."

"First thing is convincing Max to let us do Mrs. Reg's job," Lisa said.

Lisa and Carole both looked at Stevie. She had a lot of experience trying to convince Max of things. In this case they all thought it would be easy.

"Oh, Ma-ax!" she called out as he dashed by. "I've got some good news for you!"

ONCE CLASSES WERE over and their horses were groomed and fed, The Saddle Club was ready to begin the real work of the day—filling in for Mrs. Reg.

Stevie was the first one to change into street clothes, and so she was the first to arrive at Mrs. Reg's office. By the time Carole and Lisa got there, just a few seconds later, their friend had already ensconced herself in Mrs. Reg's chair and had it tilted back. Her feet were propped up on the desk.

"It's a good thing she doesn't have a cigar," Lisa teased. "She'd be trying to pretend she was some sort of mogul!"

"Ah, but I have a riding crop!" Stevie reminded her,

slapping it sharply against her thigh. "That's almost as good—maybe even better."

"Let's forget the status symbols and get to work," Carole said. "I think there's a lot to do."

Stevie removed her feet from Mrs. Reg's desk and set the chair back upright. She leaned forward and pulled the single piece of paper on the desk toward her.

"A list," she announced. "Just like Max said."

"And what does it say?" Carole asked.

"What have we gotten ourselves in for?" Lisa added.

Stevie crinkled her forehead thoughtfully.

" 'Painting, front of stable,' " she read.

The girls were quiet.

"That's a big job," Carole said.

"But it's just the *front*," Stevie said. "That's the side by the driveway. That's not big."

An image of the horse pin went through Lisa's mind. It made her realize that they just *had* to do Mrs. Reg's job, no matter how tough it might be. "You're right," she said to Stevie. "It's not big. No problem. We can get some ladders—"

Carole was swept up by their enthusiasm. "I remember when they painted the whole thing a couple of years ago. The leftover paint is stored in the utility shed by the grain shed. I'm sure there's enough left there to just do the front."

"Tomorrow," Stevie said. "We can do it after class."

"Tomorrow," they agreed. It didn't seem so hard after all.

"What's next on the list?" Lisa asked. "Redo the roof?"

"No, the next thing is much easier. It says there's going to be a new class of four beginners on Wednesday at eight o'clock. It says something here about a team and Red's going to do the class. They're also scheduled for an afternoon trail ride. Busy little kids, huh?" Stevie remarked.

"It's always a good idea to have a class start out thinking of themselves as a team," Carole said. "They work together, they learn together. I'll take care of getting the ponies ready for them tomorrow morning," she volunteered. "Dad already said he was going to have to drop me off early, so I'll be here by seven-thirty at the latest. I can saddle up four ponies first thing tomorrow."

"Check!" Stevie said. "See, this really is easy. Next says 'Buy food for Friday.'"

"I noticed that we were running low on grain when we checked the bales of hay yesterday," Lisa said.

"Well, not really low, but I suppose Mrs. Reg is just being careful."

Stevie scratched her head. The easiest way to solve this problem would be to ask Max what to order and where to order it from. However, their whole point in taking on these jobs was to keep Max from having to think about these things. *They* were being the stable managers, not he. She scratched again, harder.

"I've got it," she said. "Whenever anybody delivers anything, there are papers. Somewhere around here Mrs. Reg must have an invoice or something from the last delivery. I'll just call the same place and make the same order. If the stuff was okay the last time, it's going to be fine this time, too. The hardest part may be getting it here by Friday."

Carole looked proudly at her friend Stevie. It was nice that she could figure out how to cope with something that seemed so tricky. "Nice thinking," she said, and she meant it.

"So what's next on the list?" Lisa asked. She was beginning to get the feeling it was her turn to volunteer to solve a tricky problem.

"Wow," Stevie said, looking up from the list. "It looks like we've got a VIP coming to Pine Hollow."

"Who's that?" Lisa asked. This could be interesting.

"The French ambassador *himself*! It says here, 'Thursday, 11, Am. French. One-hour trail ride.'"

"That seems odd," Carole said. "I didn't know we had an ambassador in town."

"What's so odd about it?" Lisa challenged. "Remember when the Brazilian ambassador was here?"

Lisa had a point. Pine Hollow was located in Willow Creek, Virginia, just twenty miles from Washington, D.C. There were a lot of people who lived in town and worked in Washington. Although most of the people involved in government work were Americans, many of them did come from other countries and work in embassies and other offices like international cultural organizations. The Brazilian ambassador and his family had lived right in Willow Creek. The girls also remembered a French diplomat's daughter who had ridden at Pine Hollow for a brief time. Her name was Estelle. Lisa had befriended her and invited her to join The Saddle Club before she'd realized that Estelle was a liar. Lisa had always felt bad about what had happened. This seemed to her to be an opportunity to make it up to her friends.

"I'll take care of that," she said. "I'm getting an A in French—"

"So what else is new?" Stevie teased.

Lisa blushed and then defended herself. "Well, this time it looks like it may do me some good. Anyway, I need some practice with my French. I'll go for a trail ride with the French ambassador."

"*Merci beaucoup,*" Stevie said graciously. Then she turned to Carole. "And since Lisa is solving that problem, you get to cope with the fact that somebody named Jarvis is coming Thursday at one P.M. and wants his 'favorite horse.' That's what Mrs. Reg wrote."

"The problem with that is, Mrs. Reg always remembers who wants what horse. She assigns horses to the riders for every class," Carole said. "Max did that today, but I think we should do it starting tomorrow. I don't mind taking on that job. But I have to remember to ask Max who Mr. Jarvis's favorite horse is."

"Okay, and it makes sense for you to take on the horse assignments," Stevie said, nodding agreement. "You know the horses and the riders the best. It's a deal, and that's the last of the list."

"Piece of cake—uh, *gâteau,*" Lisa said, quickly translating "cake" into French.

Once the jobs had been assigned, it seemed to be time to begin the other part of their job as stable managers—finding Mrs. Reg's pin.

"The only place we searched yesterday was the

locker area," Carole said. "I've been thinking about it, and I think it's possible one of the cats found the pin where Veronica threw it and may have begun playing with it. You know how they are, right?"

The girls did know. They'd often seen the cats at the stable begin playing with something that wasn't a mouse. A cat could take almost anything—a pencil, marble, piece of straw—and bat it all over the place.

"The tack room!" Lisa said.

"That place is a mess!" Stevie said.

"Exactly," Carole said.

In the utility closet they found two brooms and a mop, just what they would need to probe around on the dark and shadowy floor of the tack room, where they hoped they'd find Mrs. Reg's pin. Lisa organized them. She got Carole and Stevie to begin in opposite corners, on their hands and knees, examining and sweeping every single inch of the floor as they moved toward one another. It wasn't an easy job. The tack room not only had tack hanging from every inch of wall all the way around it, it also had racks and hooks lined up in the center of the room to house saddles and bridles. There were also the upper shelves, where the specialized saddles were kept, along with the tack for the wagons and the sleigh. Lisa had decided they could omit the shelves and the loft because it was unlikely that a cat would carry the pin that high. After all, real gold was heavy, certainly heavier than a mouse. It might be fun to bat around the floor, but it would be downright dangerous for a cat to carry it up a ladder in his mouth.

"Got something!" Stevie said excitedly. She could hear the wonderful sound of metal being dragged across the old floorboards by her broom. She maneuvered the broom carefully because she couldn't see what she was pulling toward her. She could only hear it, and her ears told her it was good news. Her ears were wrong. When the broom brought her quarry into the light, Stevie saw that it wasn't a gold pin, it was a steel snaffle bit.

"False alarm," she said.

In the opposite corner, Carole took her turn. She stuck the broom back into the dark corner under what seemed to be a curtain of leather straps hanging from the wall hooks. She brought the broom back toward her. It came back empty. It wasn't actually completely empty. She had a significant dust bunny and something that looked like an old wad of gum. She also found a sponge with the remains of some saddle soap on it. She tried to imagine what would induce somebody to lose a saddle-soap sponge in the farthest, darkest corner of the tack room. She decided it must have been frustration—a feeling she suspected she was going to learn too much about in the next few days.

Lisa wasn't having any more luck than her friends. While they worked on the floor, she studied the morass of leathers and combed through the buckets of metal pieces, S-hooks, snap locks, curb chains, and the like. Tack seemed to be made up of equal parts of leather and metal, so there was an awful lot of metal in the room, but none of it was eighteen-karat gold.

The girls were too busy at their jobs to notice the arrival of Max Regnery. He cleared his throat to announce his presence.

They looked up. He stood by the door with his hands on his hips and a smile on his face.

"When you girls fill in for my mother, you really fill in! I never saw her cleaning the tack room. What happened? You couldn't find any unsuspecting riders with free time on their hands?" He laughed at his own joke.

It surprised Lisa to find that Max was actually amused by his mother's habit of assigning jobs to people who happened not to be frantically busy when she saw them.

"Very funny," Stevie said, recovering from her surprise and rising from her knees. "Actually, though, it's just that this really needed to be done, and we knew there was nobody who would do a better job than we will. So we're doing it. You wouldn't believe the dirt we're finding."

"And the sponges," Carole said.

Max looked at her quizzically. Whatever he wanted to ask or say, he decided to skip it. Some questions were best left unasked. He cleared his throat again. "Well, then, um, I'll let you girls get back to work. I'm taking a group out onto the trail. I won't be back for a while. I'll see you tomorrow."

"Oh, speaking of tomorrow," Carole said. "There's a new class beginning at eight o'clock. Did you know about that? I'll take care of tacking up their mounts when I get here early."

"I do know about them," Max said. "I have to be in town all morning. Red's taking the class for me. I wish I could be here. I like that team, but I can't. I'll tell Red you'll have the riders' horses ready. Thanks."

"No problem," Carole said. "We're just trying to be helpful."

"I can tell," Max said. "I'll be back by ten o'clock. See you all in jump class. Good-bye for now."

"Bye," Lisa said. She then turned her attention back to the buckets arrayed in front of her. Carole and Stevie reached their brooms back under the leathers. The girls worked in silence, each hoping for the sound of metal—specifically gold.

"Oh, look, the three blind mice," Veronica diAngelo said, walking into the tack room to deposit Garnet's tack on its rack. "Usually you're running *away* from work, but now that Mrs. Reg is gone, you three can't work hard enough to impress Max, can you?"

Once again Veronica had managed to astonish Lisa. It stunned her to realize how far from the truth Veronica was. Actually, she realized a second later, it was very logical. Veronica always did everything she could to get out of doing work that Mrs. Reg assigned, and also always tried, whenever it wasn't much effort, to impress Max. She naturally assumed that others had the same motivations she did. Lisa certainly didn't want to tell Veronica the truth, so she did the only other sensible thing—she agreed with her.

"You're so right, Veronica," she said. "And Max has already noticed our good work. He was so impressed that the next thing you know, he'll have us painting the stable! Want to help?"

"Hah!" Veronica said. She knew an exit line when she heard one. She was gone in a flash.

It provided a moment of laughter, but it was only a brief one. The girls had a lot of work to do and little time to do it. However, an hour later they were reluctantly concluding that the time had not been well spent. All they had to show for their work was a substantial pile of things they'd found on the floor that now had to be thrown out or put away. It wasn't what they'd had in mind when they'd begun cleaning the tack room. The worst part was that the tack room didn't look any cleaner for its careful dusting.

"Let's go, girls," Lisa said, putting her dust mop back in the utility closet.

"Fiddle-dee-dee," Stevie said as she put the broom next to Lisa's mop. "Tomorrow will be another day!"

That's just what they were all afraid of.

SINCE CAROLE LOVED *everything* about horses, it was difficult for her to choose what she loved most. High up on her list after riding them, though, were the quiet moments spent alone in a stable surrounded by horses. It made her feel more at one with them. This morning was no exception. She'd arrived at Pine Hollow before seven. Max was in town with his errands. Mrs. Reg was still at her friend's house, and Red hadn't arrived yet. The place was totally quiet, except for the comfortable sounds of horses, munching on hay, chomping on grain, the occasional stomp of a hoof on a straw-covered floor, a relaxed snort, a whinny.

"Good morning, boys and girls," Carole said, chatting easily to the ponies, who were all housed near one another. Nickel stuck his head up over the door to his stall. Carole patted his soft nose.

There were four riders coming in the beginners' class. Carole decided to tack up Nickel, Dime, Quarter, and Penny for the class. Pine Hollow, a stable filled with traditions, had the tradition of naming its ponies after coins—small change. Carole liked that tradition. The young riders always got a kick out of that, too. She was looking forward to seeing the smiles on the faces of the stable's newest riders when they arrived in forty-five minutes.

Carole began the process of tacking up the ponies. Ponies were smaller than horses; the usual definition of a pony was that it had to be less than 14.2 hands, measured at the pony's withers. A hand was four inches—the approximate width of a man's hand across the knuckles—and the .2 meant two inches. Thus a pony was no taller than fifty-eight inches from the floor to the area at the base of its mane, called the withers. Because they were relatively small, ponies were ideal mounts for young beginners. They did everything full-sized horses did; they were just smaller and less likely to frighten a new rider.

Although ponies were small, they needed the same

amount of tack as horses, so it took Carole more than half an hour to tack up four of them. When she was done, all four ponies were ready and seemed eager to meet their new riders. One by one Carole led the ponies to the paddock near the front of the stable so they could greet the riders when they arrived. They would be such a welcoming sight that Carole was sure these youngsters would be as thrilled with riding as she was. Another thing Carole loved about horses was being able to share the joy of them with others. This seemed like a wonderful opportunity to do that.

Carole climbed up onto the paddock fence and waited to welcome the new beginners. She almost wished she didn't have a class coming up right away. She was eager to introduce the kids to the ponies, show them how to climb into their saddles, teach them how to hold their riding crops and everything else that first-timers needed to know.

She could almost see the smiles on their faces and hear their excited giggles. Carole loved to watch little girls and boys in their brand-new riding clothes—boots without a scratch, pants that are a little loose so the girls can grow into them—actually sitting in a saddle for the first time. Carole sighed contentedly just thinking about it all. She was so involved in her own daydream that she never even saw Red O'Malley walk over to her, followed by four extremely tall men in riding clothes.

"Morning, Carole," Red said. "Max told me you were taking care of tacking up horses for the new class today."

"Yep," Carole said proudly. "I've got Nickel, Penny, Quarter, and Dime all ready and raring to go. The kids ought to be here any minute." She looked at her watch. It was already eight o'clock. "Funny. They should already be here."

One of the men standing near Red cleared his throat. "They *are* already here," he said.

Carole looked at him. A fog began to clear, and she didn't much like what she saw. In front of her were four very large men. Behind her were four very small ponies. This wasn't a class of beginning children riders. These were definitely grown-ups—and very big ones at that. Then she remembered that Mrs. Reg's note had said something about a "team," and Max had used the same word. One more look and she didn't have to ask the question. She knew what the word "team" meant. These men were basketball players from the local professional team. They were well over six feet tall. One of them was probably seven feet tall, and Carole had saddled up the stable's smallest ponies for them!

She wanted to die.

One of the men started laughing.

"I thought we were supposed to do the riding, but if these little fellows need to go somewhere, I guess we could carry them," another said.

Red laughed, too.

"I'd thought—" Carole began, but she couldn't go on. Everybody knew what she'd thought. She didn't need to explain. She just felt terribly embarrassed. She also could imagine what her father—a big basketball fan—was going to say when he heard about her mistake.

Since dying didn't seem to be a real option right then, Carole decided that her only other choice was to correct her mistake. She slid down from the fence and unhitched two ponies to return them to their stalls. Then, at just exactly the right minute, Stevie and Lisa arrived. One glance and they knew what they had to do. They each took a lead rope and followed Carole into the stable. Without discussion the girls saddled up Pine Hollow's four tallest horses and had them hitched in the paddock within ten minutes.

All images of the joyful faces of happy children and

the gleeful giggles of young learners had fled from Carole's mind. The only thing she wanted to see was the backs of four very tall men on four very tall horses disappearing around the far side of the stable where she couldn't see them laughing at her silly mistake. Carole didn't like to appear ridiculous, but she thought she'd done an awfully good job of it that morning. She cringed as she held the horses' leads while the men mounted, and she shuddered with relief when Red finally led the group to the ring.

"Thank you," she whispered to her friends.

"Oh, you're welcome," Lisa said.

"No problem," Stevie agreed. "I got the feeling that this was the funniest thing that had happened to those guys in a long time. They *loved* it."

Carole gave her a withering look. Stevie realized that Carole did not see the humor. She hadn't loved it at all.

"Shouldn't we be tacking up our own horses for class?" Lisa asked.

"And *untacking* the ponies," Carole said pointedly. Not only had she made an awful mistake, but she'd also caused herself and her friends a lot of unnecessary work. No matter how funny the men thought it was and no matter how lightly Lisa and Stevie took it, the whole thing upset Carole a lot.

She was calmer, but still upset, when her class began. On Wednesdays they began their day with drill work, followed by jump class. These were two things Carole loved. She loved the precision of trying to make her horse do just exactly what she told him to do so he would be coordinated with the other horses. It was a challenge for her horse, Starlight, who tended to be a little resentful of very structured activities, but that was a challenge Carole was usually willing to meet. This day she found she wasn't so willing, and as a result, Starlight was even less willing. She had to take him out of the drill and work with him alone until he was calmed down, but she knew that it wasn't Starlight who needed calming; it was Carole.

Jump class was even worse. By then Max was back and he'd heard about Carole's mix-up from Red. Since the basketball players thought it was funny, Max thought it was funny. He thought it was funny enough to tease her about it so that although only a few people had known at the beginning of the class, by the time Carole had been asked to take Starlight over a few jumps that were just one inch high, everybody knew and was laughing.

"They're not laughing at you," Stevie said. "They're laughing at the situation."

It didn't make Carole feel any better. By lunchtime

she found herself actually looking forward to painting the stable. At least she could be on a ladder so high above everybody else that she couldn't see them laugh.

WHEN THREE O'CLOCK came around, The Saddle Club groomed their horses and put them back into their stalls for the day. Class was done, it was time for the real work to begin.

Stevie had a list. It read: paint, brushes, ladders. Lisa also had a list. It read: paint (red and white), pans, brushes, ladder, turpentine, hats, drop cloths, tape.

Carole looked at both lists. It confirmed her suspicion that Lisa was a better list maker than Stevie.

"I'm sure all this stuff is in the utility shed," Carole said. The three girls went there and found that Carole was right.

Carole found the cans of paint and stacked them for ease of carrying. Lisa found the pans, brushes, turpentine, tape, hats, and drop cloths—

"What do we need drop cloths for?" Stevie asked. "We're painting outside, not inside. Do we really have to protect the ground?"

"You never know," Lisa said, sounding very much as if she did, in fact, know. Then, to prove it, she spread one of the drop cloths out, put all the equipment onto it, and then folded up the corners of the drop cloth so she could use it as a carrying bag. Stevie thought that sometimes Lisa was almost *too* organized for her own good.

Stevie spotted the folding ladder and picked it up. It was long and awkward, but it wasn't awfully heavy, and she found that as long as she held it in the middle, she could manage it. The three girls walked together back toward the stable.

As they walked, it occurred to Stevie that it was just about perfect painting weather. The sun was bright; the sky was cloudless. It wasn't too hot and it wasn't humid. There was something about the lovely summer day that made Stevie feel good. She wasn't alone either. Out of the corner of her eye, she spotted Pepper, an old retired horse, positively frolicking in his pasture.

"Oh, look at that!" she said, turning to watch.

Her sudden movement accomplished several things. It gave Stevie a better view of Pepper, but it also made the ladder turn with her, knocking both of her friends off their feet.

"Oomph!"

"Watch—"

"Oh, sorry," Stevie said when she saw what she had done. She turned back, much more carefully than she'd turned around in the first place.

"That's quite a weapon," Lisa remarked, looking warily at the ladder.

"In the right hands," Carole said pointedly.

"You guys okay?" Stevie asked. She really hadn't meant to hurt her friends, and she felt bad about it.

"We will be as long as we don't walk next to you again!" Lisa said. She wasn't hurt, but she was more than a little annoyed that Stevie's mistake had made her drop everything she was carrying, and now three painter's hats were blowing across the pasture toward Pepper.

"I'll get them!" Stevie offered, once again swinging around so she could see where they were going. Lisa and Carole dived for cover—this time managing to get out of the way of the swirling ladder.

"*I'll* get the hats," Lisa said. "And Stevie, you walk ahead—*way* ahead."

Sheepishly Stevie agreed.

# 5

"LOOK, ALL WE have to do is put some white paint on the white parts and some red paint on the red parts. What's so hard about that?"

Stevie's own words echoed in her head. It had all seemed so easy when she said it, but now she appeared to be very busy putting the white parts on the red parts and vice versa, and the overall effect was definitely more *pink* than anything else.

"Grrrrr!" she commented.

Lisa and Carole were beneath her at ground level. Stevie had claimed the ladder, thinking it would be fun to be up high. What it really was, was harder. Every time she needed something, she had to step down, and the ladder wobbled in a very unpleasant way.

"Trouble up there?" Lisa asked, looking at Stevie's scrowl.

"I'd like to be able to say that I'm seeing red," Stevie said sardonically. "However, it seems to be more like pink. . . ."

Lisa stepped back and looked up. Stevie had a point. The stable was definitely taking on a pink hue, and that wasn't what was supposed to happen.

"I did the white and then I did the red, but the white got mixed in with the red and the red with the white, and I think I'd better not make any long-term plans to be a house painter."

Lisa squinted to see what was causing the problem. She was such a logical person that she didn't always understand when other people weren't as logical as she was. Stevie was a special problem in that regard! Then she figured it out.

"Masking tape," she said. "You need masking tape."

"I do?" Stevie asked.

"Definitely," Lisa said. "See, first you paint all the red parts, more or less trying to avoid the white ones, but if you get some red on those, it's okay. When the red is dry, you put tape around the edges of the white and you paint the white. So then, if you slosh a little over the edges, all you're painting is the tape, not the red. When the white is dry, you remove the tape and *bingo*, it's perfect."

"It is?" Stevie was not convinced.

"Try it," Lisa said. She handed up a roll of tape.

Stevie looked at the parts that Lisa had already done, and she had to admit that they looked an awful lot better than what she was working on. She put down the brush with white paint and picked up the one with red paint. She began again, blotting out all the pink with red. It looked better immediately. Stevie painted with renewed enthusiasm.

"Well, if it isn't the three blind mice again," Veronica said icily. "Scurrying like crazy, trying to impress Max again, huh?"

"Watch it, Veronica," Stevie said from above. "We're armed." She held her red paintbrush menacingly above Veronica's head. The idea of red splatters on her designer breeches and jacket was more than Veronica could stand. She dashed off. The Saddle Club was not sorry to see her go. They resumed their work.

Lisa found that she had developed a rhythm to her strokes. Up down, up down, shift to the right, up down, up down, time to refill the brush. Up down, up down . . . It went quickly enough, and the results

49

were good. The trouble was that it was tiring for her arm. She shifted the paintbrush to her left hand and resumed her work. That was okay for a while. Then she spent more time taping around the white sections on parts of the red that were already dry. That was when a sound caught her ear. It was the playful whinny of a horse romping in a paddock. Then she remembered.

"Diablo," she said. Carole and Stevie looked at her. "I left him in the paddock after class," she explained. "He seemed to need more of a cool-down than I had time to give him, so I just set him loose in the paddock. I thought that would help."

"He's probably cooled down by now," Carole said. "Why don't you take a break and bring him into the stable."

Those were the very words Lisa's weary arm had been waiting to hear. That way she could take a break, but still be doing something useful. "Okay," she agreed.

Diablo sniffed curiously as Lisa approached him with a lead rope. At first she thought he was sniffing at her, but then she realized that the smell of paint seemed to be alerting him. Lisa had often wondered what was on a horse's mind, and she did so again. Horses often had early warning systems that told them something dangerous was around, even when there wasn't anything dangerous at all. Prancer's fear of cats was like that. Diablo seemed to be nervous about the smell of paint. Lisa spoke to calm him.

"Don't worry, boy, there's nothing to fear. We're just doing a little work for Mrs. Reg. It won't be long, and then imagine how nice the stable is going to look—at least from the front. Your home is going to be so beautiful that you'll be proud to invite your friends to come see it."

She knew the horse couldn't understand a word she was saying, but she also knew that he understood her tone of voice and that was all that mattered. Reassured, Diablo followed her to the stable. She kept chatting all the while.

"And when I put you in your stall, I'm going to give you some fresh hay and water, and that'll be so delicious and smell so good, you won't even notice the paint, will you?"

Lisa was totally occupied with her chattering. She was too occupied to notice what Stevie was doing on top of the ladder as she and Diablo approached. Stevie had peeled out a yard-long piece of masking tape. It was too long and immediately became an unruly tangle. As she tried to untangle it, it stuck onto the cloth she'd been using to wipe her hands and her brushes. Then the tape attached to the brush with red paint.

"Oh, drat!" Stevie said, trying to loosen everything from the mass of tape.

Lisa didn't see any of this. Diablo saw it all. Lisa tugged at his lead rope, bringing him right between the legs of the folding ladder where Stevie was perched at just the moment when Stevie shook the sticky tangled mess of tape, rag, and brush most vigorously. It was all Diablo could take. He didn't exactly rear, though he came close to it. He shied and he bucked. It was just enough to jiggle the ladder seriously, and when that happened, something else happened, too. Two paint buckets, once carefully balanced on the ladder's shelf, became unbalanced and toppled over.

Lisa had already passed under the ladder. Most of Diablo had not. Much to the horse's dismay—to say nothing of the girls'—his rear half was drenched by the toppled red and white paint. It was all he could take. He bolted. Lisa was so astonished that she simply let go of the lead rope and watched helplessly while he fled right through the stable, out the other side, and into the paddock at the back of the stable. Normally that would be enough to contain him, but not in his frightened state. Diablo took one look at the paddock fence and flew right over it.

Stevie growled again. Lisa hollered "Stop him!" but there was nobody there to stop him, and even if there had been, he was too frightened to be stopped. When it came to horse trouble, Carole was the most logical thinker in the group. She put down her paintbrush.

"I'll take Starlight out and catch Diablo," she said. "He'll stop running pretty soon, and I know he's going to be easy to find."

"Sure," Lisa said, dismayed. "How many horses are there out in the field dressed as a clown?"

"He did look pretty funny, you know," Stevie said, trying to emphasize the absurdity of it all. The humor was lost on Lisa. She gave Stevie a withering look. Stevie realized this might not be the best time to try to joke about what had happened. From the look on Lisa's face, it seemed that sometime in the future— like fifty years into the future—would be a better time. She turned her paint buckets back upright, took her brush in her hand, and resumed painting. She reminded herself that as long as Carole was going to fetch Diablo, the best thing she could do was paint. Lisa didn't say anything. She just picked up her paintbrush and got back to work, too.

Carole took off her painter's hat and went to Starlight's stall. She was always glad for an excuse to ride her horse, and this seemed an especially nice time, since it gave her an opportunity to be away from a guilty Stevie and an angry Lisa. She hoped they'd both be in better moods by the time she got back.

She didn't want to take the time to tack up Starlight. She decided to ride him bareback. She slipped a bridle on him, led him to the rear door of the stable—*away* from the painters—and hopped onto his back. Riding Starlight bareback was always a special joy. It made her feel closer to her horse and closer to the origins of riding. After all, the first riders had hardly had choices between English and Western saddles, pads and blankets. They just sat on their horses' backs and rode. Now that was what Carole was doing, too. She felt the strong and supple horse beneath her, and with every step she pulled farther and farther away from everything that had gone wrong—the ponies and the basketball players, the dreadful drill class, the embarrassing jump class, the miserable painting job they were doing, the horrible paint spill on poor old Diablo.

Starlight seemed to sense Carole's need for freedom and liberation from the less-than-perfect day. He took a deep breath and lengthened his stride, moving more quickly, more surely, as his rider directed him.

It didn't take Carole long to spot Diablo. For one thing, he was the only red-and-white horse in the field. For another, he was the only horse in the field at all. He seemed unaware of the new color he'd taken on, and he was munching quietly at the sweet grass. Starlight picked up a trot and approached him. Diablo lifted his head when he heard the other horse approaching. Apparently that was enough quiet munching for Diablo. Another possibility was that he recognized Carole as one of the people who had covered him with paint, and he didn't want anything more to do with her. He moved away.

Carole drew in Starlight's reins. He slowed to a walk while Carole thought about the situation. If Diablo didn't want to be caught, she and Starlight had two choices. The first was to be patient and wait for Diablo to change his mind, approaching him slowly all the time. The other was to try to chase him down. Carole opted for patience. Starlight stopped about twenty feet from Diablo. Diablo seemed a little nervous at first, but once he became convinced he wasn't being chased, he turned his attention to the grass at his feet. Carole had Starlight take another few steps. Diablo took a few steps, too. Carole stopped. She waited and then she tried again. This time she and Starlight closed the gap to fifteen feet. She waited and tried again. Starlight took three steps, Diablo took only two. It was slow, but it was working. Carole waited some more and tried again. She found that if she watched Diablo's ears very carefully, she could tell when he was relaxed enough for her to approach him just a little bit.

She was less than six feet from the horse when a group of riders appeared at the edge of the field. Diablo's ears perked up alertly. He lifted his head. This horse had already had as much trauma as he could take for one day. Five more horses, with riders who might or might not be planning something for him, were just too much for Diablo. He took off and fled, and at that moment all of Carole's patience fled, too. She took the only other option open to her. She raced after him.

Diablo tore across the field, challenging the trail riders by racing right at them. At first Carole saw only that there were five riders and that one of them was Red O'Malley. All of her concentration was on the red-and-white-splattered horse ahead of her. Then the sound of laughter distracted her enough to make her look at exactly who those riders were. Her second look was all it took, for she could see that all of them, except Red, were very, very tall. The beginners' class of basketball players had apparently talked Red into a follow-up trail ride, and they were enjoying themselves immensely—at Carole's expense.

That was when Carole stopped seeing red and white speckles and began to see only red. She was only trying to do the very best job she could, and it seemed that the harder she tried, the bigger mistakes she made and the more these men ended up laughing at her. She was furious!

Beneath her, Starlight felt a sudden change in her mood and her position. Starlight always tried to please Carole, and so he wanted to do what he thought she wanted. He didn't always do the right thing, but this time he did. Without further urging, he began moving faster and more surely in pursuit of the frantic Diablo. Once Starlight was committed, it didn't take long. Carole and Starlight flew past the laughing riders. She never looked back—just concentrated totally on the loose horse in front of her. Diablo tried dodging, he tried running, he tried doubling back. None of it worked. Starlight had him in his sights, and Carole was totally determined to win. Within a few minutes Starlight had come up alongside the fleeing bay. Carole reached over and grabbed the dangling lead rope. Without further instruction Starlight did exactly the right thing. He watched Diablo out of one eye and matched his own pace to Diablo's. Carole tugged gently on the lead rope. Diablo wanted to run some more, but he was a well-trained horse and knew a sharp signal when he felt one. He slowed. Starlight slowed as well. Diablo slowed some more. So did Starlight. Soon Starlight and Diablo were walking. Carole began speaking to the frightened horse.

"Don't worry, boy. We're going to take care of you. We'll get you back to the stable and see if we can't get some of that nasty paint off you. We'll get you some hay and some grain and a nice bucket of fresh water. You'll have your friends nearby, and not a one of them will dare make fun of you. Nobody's going to laugh at you at all."

Diablo listened to Carole. Even though he couldn't understand the words, he understood the tone. Carole spoke to him the entire way back to the stable—even as she passed Red and the basketball players. She knew that as long as she was talking to the horse, they wouldn't try to say anything to her. As she passed, however, she did hear Red explaining her chatter to the tall men.

"She's calming the horse down," Red said, "and she knows exactly what she's doing."

"She *does*?" one of the men asked, sounding rather astonished. The other three began laughing.

For the second time that day, Carole wanted to die. Instantly.

CAROLE WENT DIRECTLY to the stalls with Starlight and Diablo. She called out to Stevie and Lisa to let them know that she was back and had Diablo. She didn't want to be anywhere in public where anyone, especially four basketball players, one head stable hand, and one stable owner, might see her and start laughing at all the foolish things she'd done all day long. Animals were more forgiving than people. The horses, even Diablo, seemed happy for her company.

She removed Starlight's bridle, gave him a quick brushing, and set him loose in his stall. She'd already groomed him once that day, and that should be enough. Diablo was going to be more of a challenge. She found some old rags and began working on the paint. It was oil-based, fast-drying outdoor paint. It didn't want to come off at all. She knew she could use turpentine on it, but that stuff was very abrasive and could harm the horse's skin. Since Diablo tended to have sensitive skin, she thought it was a bad idea. Moreover, turpentine was very flammable, and she didn't like the idea of using something very flammable in the stable where fire was always a danger. Finally, the thought of the strong, unpleasant odor filling the stable was enough to convince her not to use turpentine. She rubbed, she washed, she brushed, she combed. She actually got some paint off, but not much. After working on it for fifteen minutes, she decided that it would be no worse tomorrow, when she could work on it outdoors and use some turpentine carefully.

"Sorry about that, Diablo," she said, patting his shoulder affectionately. "For now you're just going to have to live with it. Tomorrow Stevie and Lisa and I will begin work on your make-over. We'll get you back to a nice glistening brown, okay?"

He nuzzled her and tickled her neck. "If that's an apology for your misbehavior, I accept it," she said, and hugged him back. At least Diablo didn't seem to be inclined to laugh at her. She gave him fresh hay and water and a ration of grain for his supper.

She found the four basketball players' horses in the paddock by the stable's rear door, waiting to be untacked and put up for the night. When there was work to be done, Carole was always glad to do it. She knew her friends could use help with the painting, but Carole just didn't feel ready to be with other people right then. She felt more like staying with the horses. She wondered where Red had disappeared to, but when she heard his voice in Max's office, she knew he would be particularly happy to have her help. Max and Red were having a loud conversation, making plans for the rest of the week. It seemed that The Saddle Club members weren't the only people who missed Mrs. Reg.

Without further hesitation Carole began her next job. One by one, she took the horses into the stalls. Each one had to be untacked, groomed, watered, and fed. Since it was evening and they wouldn't be going out of the stable again until morning, it had to be done right. Carole was good at this kind of work, but there weren't many shortcuts when it came to taking good care of horses. It was almost an hour before she could return to her friends. They would understand. At least she hoped they would.

When the last horse was groomed and fed and put up for the night, she was ready to go back to the painting. It was twilight. Carole hated to think about how much more work there would be to do. Three girls simply couldn't paint the entire front of stable in a few hours—even three very determined girls. They would have to work into the night and be at the stable even earlier the next morning. And then there would be tomorrow night. . . .

The thought alone exhausted Carole.

"Here I come," she announced to her friends as she walked toward the stable's front door. "Give me a brush. What needs to be done most?"

"Nothing," Lisa said as Carole emerged from the stable into the dim twilight. "It's all done."

"Very funny," Carole said.

"No joke," said Stevie.

Carole looked. The sky was darkening, but it wasn't so dark that she couldn't see the whole job had been finished. The front of the stable was now a beautiful deep red with a sparkling white trim. The job *was* done. The ladders, buckets, brushes, drop cloths, and hats were nowhere in sight.

"How could the two of you do all that work by yourselves?" Carole asked. She was totally astonished.

"We had some help," Lisa said.

"Santa's elves?" Carole asked. "It's not exactly the season, you know."

"No, more like the Jolly Green Giants—four of them in fact," Stevie said.

That could only mean one thing. "The basketball players?" she asked.

"You won't believe how high they could reach without even using a ladder!" Lisa said.

"You are amazing, Stevie. How did you talk those clowns into helping you?"

"I didn't have anything to do with it," Stevie said. "It was all you. When they saw how much work you were doing around here, they said that any place that inspired such devotion certainly deserved to have their help. They spent more than an hour doing all the hardest parts of the painting. Without them we'd be here until midnight. We have you to thank for their help."

"Me?" Carole asked. "I don't understand. They spent the whole day laughing at my silly mistakes."

"No," Lisa said. "They spent the whole day admiring what you were trying to do. They liked it so much, they want to sign up the whole rest of the basketball team for lessons. Max is going wild trying to figure out when he's going to fit them into the schedule, but Red is trying to talk him into buying some taller horses!"

Carole shook her head in disbelief. It was hard to imagine how so much good could come from one really dumb mistake. She was simply too tired to take it all in. It would have to wait for another day.

"ALL RIGHT, THEN, that's it," Stevie said—much more positively than she felt. "We all have our assignments, let's begin the day."

Carole snapped a salute at her and clicked her heels.

"Am I that bad?" Stevie asked sheepishly.

Lisa nodded.

Stevie was finding that when three girls were trying to equal one woman, it wasn't easy in more ways than one. It wasn't easy because it was hard to do the job, and it particularly wasn't easy because it was a strain on their friendship. Each of them was nervous that she was going to mess up and it would be her fault. There was so much to do and it was *so* important.

This morning, for example, Stevie had to figure out how to order food for the horses. She'd made the job sound light when she took it on, but the truth was, she wasn't at all sure about what to do, and she didn't want to goof.

Lisa's job could be even trickier. She'd volunteered to skip jump class to take the French ambassador out on a trail ride. The U.S. had pretty good relationships with France, and it seemed unlikely that anything Lisa would do, or not do, was going to change that. Still, it was a big responsibility.

Although Carole's job wouldn't affect international relations, or cost Pine Hollow a lot of money if she made a mistake, it was in its way even trickier than her friends' jobs. Carole had taken on the task of assigning horses to riders. She had already unfolded a giant chart she'd made last night to keep track of the names of riders and horses and class hours. She spread the chart out on Mrs. Reg's desk and looked pointedly at Stevie, who relinquished the chair. Carole instantly began scribbling on her chart. Lisa hurried to a quiet spot in the locker area and pulled out her French phrase book. Stevie headed for the feed shed.

She knew that feed for horses consisted primarily of hay and grain, both of which could be a fire hazard. She didn't exactly understand what caused spontaneous combustion in bales of hay, but she'd seen the result in a barn fire once and never wanted to see it again. Grain was a fire hazard because it was dusty and the dust particles could almost hang in the air. In the case of a fire—or even a spark that might start one—the dust particles themselves would burn, and that burning would be explosive. For those reasons most stables, including Pine Hollow, stored their feed in a separate shed. No matter how careful people were, accidents happened. Keeping the potential accident a distance from the horses made the stable itself safer for the animals.

Stevie opened the door to the feed shed and turned on the light. Bags, barrels, and bales were piled neatly everywhere. The place was pretty full, so it seemed odd that Mrs. Reg wanted to order more for Friday, but who was Stevie to disagree with something on Mrs. Reg's list?

And who was Stevie to figure out what Mrs. Reg wanted to order? And how on earth was she going to do it?

She sat down on a bale of hay and began chewing on a fingernail. It didn't taste very good, and it didn't help her thinking. She stopped chewing on the nail and looked around, hoping to pull an answer out of thin air. And she did.

For there, fastened to a clipboard that was hanging from a hook by the door to the shed, was a piece of pink paper. On a hunch, Stevie walked over to look at it. It was an invoice, dated just a month earlier. At the top of the piece of paper, it gave the name of the place that had delivered the feed: Connor Hay & Grain. Then there was an address and a phone number. Better still, it said at the top: *Standing Order*. That meant that this was probably just about exactly what Mrs. Reg ordered every time she called.

"Bingo!" Stevie announced. She took the clipboard down off the hook and dashed back to Mrs. Reg's office, remembering to turn off the light and lock the door behind her. Maybe it wasn't so hard to be Mrs. Reg after all.

"BONJOUR," LISA SAID, practicing her welcome to the French ambassador. "*Je m'appelle Lisa Atwood.*" Introducing herself wouldn't be so hard. The hard part was going to be chatting about horseback riding, or international affairs—whatever the man wanted. She'd spent more than two hours the night before boning up on her horseback-riding vocabulary. She'd made herself a list, but she'd worked so hard on memorizing it that she hoped she wouldn't have to refer to it too much. Saddle, for instance, was *selle*. Sidesaddle was *selle d'amazone.* She didn't actually think she was going to need to talk about sidesaddles because she'd never even ridden one, but she was interested to learn that the name in French was connected with the women warriors, the Amazons. Perhaps she could work it into a conversation, although she didn't know the word for "warrior," and that would make it hard to talk about.

Lisa found that she did get mixed up between horses and hairs. In French the word for horse was *cheval* and more than one horse was *chevaux.* Hair, on the other hand, was *cheveux.* She certainly hoped she didn't goof and ask the poor ambassador if he wanted to ride any hairs!

A car pulled up to the stable. It was ten-fifteen. All the riders, plus Max and Red, were in the jump class. This could only be the French ambassador. When a distinguished-looking, middle-aged man stepped out of the car, Lisa knew she was right. She took a deep breath and went to work.

"*Bonjour,*" she began. "*Je m'appelle Lisa Atwood.*"

There was no question about it, the look on the man's face was complete surprise. Then he smiled. Lisa was terribly proud of herself.

"*Bonjour, Lisa,*" he said, offering his hand for a shake.

They had definitely gotten off on the right foot—or *pied*, as the French would say. Lisa began her carefully memorized words of welcome and explanation. She took the ambassador to the locker area and told him she would be putting *une selle* on his *cheval* and would meet him by the *porte d'ecurie en dix minutes*. That would give him ten minutes to get to the stable door. He said *merci beaucoup*, so Lisa figured that would be fine.

Quickly she tacked up Barq for herself and Delilah for the ambassador. Delilah was a beautiful palomino mare, and she was sure the man would be pleased to be able to ride her. Delilah was also very gentle, so no matter whether the ambassador was a good rider or not, Delilah would be a good horse for him.

The man was ready and waiting for Lisa when she appeared with his horse. Then came a tricky part. Pine Hollow's riders sometimes joked that the place was built on traditions, because it had an awful lot of them. One of the most important, however, was the good-luck horseshoe. Every rider was supposed to touch the horseshoe nailed up by the door before going out on a ride. No rider at Pine Hollow had ever been badly hurt, and tradition held that it was because of the horseshoe.

Lisa couldn't manage a long explanation, but she

could demonstrate. She mounted Barq, touched the shoe, and looked at the ambassador. *"Fer à cheval pour bonne chance,"* she said. He smiled at her and touched it as well. He'd understood! She was very pleased with herself. She felt as though she were riding on a new high as she led the way out the door and off to the trail through the field. She waved gaily at her jump classmates when they passed by.

*"Au revoir,"* Stevie called. Lisa and the ambassador both shouted *"Au revoir"* back at her. That was French for good-bye, and it really meant "until we see one another again." That sounded so much nicer than "good-bye." Lisa found herself beginning to love the French language. That feeling made it much easier to speak in it, too. And as she spoke, she found that she lost some of her self-consciousness. Pretty soon she and her charge were chatting easily about various things that Lisa hadn't even known she knew how to say. She was, in fact, having fun, and so was the man who was riding with her.

She wanted to tell him about The Saddle Club. She had the feeling that this nice man would really understand. He was a good rider, and he was very friendly. Since those were the two basic requirements for membership, she wanted to explain it.

*"Moi et mes amies,"* she began. *"Nous avons un,* uh,

*une*, oh, drat, *une* . . ." She groped for something that would be like the word "club" in French, but nothing came to her. "I just can't remember the word for 'club' in French," she said, and then shrugged sheepishly to convey to him that she was at a loss.

"I can't remember it, either," the man said. "But I suspect it's something like *club* or *associacion*. Anyway, why don't we try English for a while?"

It took Lisa about eight very long seconds to register what she'd just heard and what it really sounded like. In those eight seconds, she realized that she'd heard English spoken, and it wasn't accented English, unless you counted a pleasant southern Virginia drawl.

"You're not the French ambassador—you're not even French!" she stammered.

"Of course I am," the man said. "I'm Michael French. I thought you knew."

Mrs. Reg's list had said it was the French ambassador who was coming to ride. How could she have made a mistake like that? Then Lisa realized it wasn't Mrs. Reg who had made the mistake. It was The Saddle Club. Mrs. Reg had written "Thursday, 11, Am. French." She hadn't meant Am. French. She'd meant eleven A.M., and she'd just written it a little oddly.

Lisa wanted to disappear. Right then and there she wanted to find a way to be swallowed up by the earth. How could she have been so silly? There she'd been, speaking sort of pidgin French to this poor man, who really only wanted to ride a horse!

"Oh, no," she groaned. "I'm—" She couldn't even think of the words in English! "I can't—I mean, it's so—"

"Don't worry!" the man said. He actually sounded cheerful, which struck Lisa as odd. "I'm really very flattered," he went on. "See, I work for the government in the State Department. I would like nothing more than to be an ambassador. The fact that you thought I was one already—well, you can imagine, I've loved every minute of it. Besides, as you surely know, French is the language of diplomacy, and mine's been getting a little rusty, stuck in an office in Washington as I am. You gave me a chance to speak in French. It was terrific. I only expected to learn something about horseback riding. I got twice the value for my money!"

"You're being awfully nice about this," Lisa said, now not so eager to disappear into the earth. "In fact, I think you're giving me a lesson in diplomacy."

"Oh, but I mean it," Mr. French insisted. "And now

that we've brushed up my languages, let's see if you can do as well with the riding instruction, which I'm sure will be a little easier in our native tongue. Just exactly what was it you were trying to tell me about the Amazon River and women who ride horses?"

Lisa tried to stifle her giggle, but she couldn't contain it. "I guess I ride better than I speak French," she said when she could talk. "That has to do with side-saddles."

Much to Lisa's surprise and pleasure, Mr. French seemed genuinely interested in learning about side-saddles and everything else she could tell him about riding and horses. When they finally returned to Pine Hollow an hour and a half later, they'd had a great ride, and they'd both learned an awful lot. Mr. French had learned about horses. Lisa had learned about people.

"CAN YOU GET the order here by Friday?" Stevie asked. The man at the other end of the phone wasn't too happy with the question.

"We just delivered there. You need more already?"

"Look, I'm just filling in for Mrs. Reg," Stevie said. Although she usually felt that being devious was the way to accomplish something, in this case she suspected that straightforward begging was going to be the most effective. "She was called to the bedside of a very sick friend who needed her to nurse her, wipe her brow, feed her gruel—" Stevie wondered briefly what gruel was, but it sounded like something somebody who was sick would eat. "Selflessly she left her family and her home to be with her friend and asked that we do a few meager chores in her absence. Her thoughts were with those who needed her the most: her friend and the horses. Can we let them go without, just because Mrs. Reg—"

"All right, all right! Stop already!" the man practically hollered into the telephone. "You've got me crying, miss. We'll deliver. The stuff will be there Friday morning just like you asked. You may or may not have a future as a stable manager, but I'm sure you could get a job on a soap opera. . . ."

"Thanks for your help," Stevie said. "I know Mrs. Reg will be pleased and grateful and . . ."

"Yeah, and she'll wipe my brow and give me gruel when I get sick, huh?"

"I'll leave a note for her," Stevie said.

When they hung up, Stevie reflected on the conversation. Then she had a little laugh to herself, confident that in the office at Connor Hay & Grain there was a man who was doing exactly the same thing. The two of them had seen exactly eye to eye, and it had been fun.

Stevie sighed contentedly. Being a stable manager had its rewards.

CAROLE WAS VERY proud of her charts. It wasn't easy to keep track of who was riding which horse when, but it was important. For one thing, it was a way of keeping track of what riders were out. For another, and really more important as far as Carole was concerned, it was a way of telling how long each horse was working. Horses couldn't spend all day every day with riders on their backs. Just like people, they needed time to rest and recuperate. Mrs. Reg always tried to arrange it so that no horse spent more than four hours a day in class. Carole thought she could manage that, too.

Charts weren't all of the job, though. The harder part was pleasing the riders. In Red's beginner class, three of the girls had wanted to ride Delilah. Carole was almost relieved when she saw that Lisa had taken the mare for the French ambassador. That way the girls couldn't fight over her. Instead they began fighting about which one of them was going to ride Patch. Carole solved that problem by talking louder than the squabbling young riders. She put them each on horses they hadn't ridden before and told each—in a whisper—that they were getting the best horse. That at least worked.

Now in a quiet moment (because all the squabbling little girls were in class with Red), Carole turned to her other job for the day, which was to look for the pin some more, though she was becoming more and more certain they would not be able to find it. Carole decided it was time to make a careful examination of the stable area, particularly the wide aisle that ran between the stalls in the U-shaped stable. There was always a layer of straw on the floor there, and that was just the sort of camouflage a gold pin could use to hide out.

Carole picked up a pitchfork and began working on the straw methodically. She picked up a forkful and shook it, hoping to find a gold pin dropping out of the mass of straw. Then, when nothing gold fell out, she put down that forkful and picked up another. By the

time she'd picked up eight forkfuls, she'd decided
it was almost impossible that this would work. Still,
she didn't have a better idea. She picked up her ninth
forkful. Then her tenth and her eleventh . . .

"Don't look at me that way," she said to Starlight,
who was gazing at her curiously over the door to his
stall. Starlight didn't have anything to say to that. He
pulled his head back in. Carole continued her work in
silence.

Most of the horses were now out on trail rides or
busy in classes. The stable was unusually quiet, and
Carole was hopeful that it would make it easier for her
to hear the very welcome *thump* of a solid gold pin
hitting the wide boards of the stable floor. No matter
how much she listened, though, there was no such
*thump*.

There was, however, another sound, and it was
coming from the tack room. Carole stopped her work
and listened. Then she was sure. There was definitely
some sniffling going on. It didn't sound like an allergy
or a cold, either. It sounded very unhappy.

Carole propped the pitchfork up against a beam and
peered into the tack room. Somebody was in there crying and probably wanted to be alone. Carole didn't
intend to interrupt unless she seemed to be needed.

One look and Carole knew she was needed. There

sat May Grover, one of Pine Hollow's young riders and a particular favorite of Carole's. May was crying her eyes out.

"Could you use a friend?" Carole asked.

"I don't have any," May said, tears streaming down her face, but the look in her eyes said that, more than anything, she wanted Carole to come be with her.

Carole came in and perched on the bench next to May. She reached into her jeans pocket and found a tissue. Silently she offered it to the young girl. While May blew her nose, Carole recalled a conversation she'd overheard earlier between May and her friend Jessica. Before class May had been telling the other young rider in no uncertain terms just exactly how to do something, and Jessica hadn't reacted kindly. Carole thought she recalled, in fact, that Jessica had told May just exactly what to do with the rest of her life. It hadn't been nice, but even best friends had arguments sometimes. Carole hadn't taken it very seriously. May apparently had.

May was wise and strong. At least that was how she always appeared. As a result, her classmates sometimes thought she was a little bossy. She knew an awful lot about horses and tended to lecture her friends. Being right wasn't always enough. That was something

Carole had learned long ago, and she had the feeling that it was May's turn to learn it now.

"Is it what Jessica said?" Carole asked May.

May looked at Carole in surprise, totally unaware of the fact that Carole had heard the argument. Carole had a funny feeling then. There was one person who always seemed to be aware of what was going on among the young riders, even when they had no idea that she was aware of it at all, and that was Mrs. Reg. Now Carole and her friends were trying, in their own way, to replace Mrs. Reg, and Carole was finding that she was replacing her in more than one way. In her absence Carole was somehow becoming a person who knew what was going on.

What would Mrs. Reg do if she were here, Carole wondered. In the first place, she wouldn't let on that she knew what had happened. In the second place, she'd tell a story. Mrs. Reg had a story for every occasion. It was her way of telling the riders that she knew what was happening and of offering advice very indirectly. In fact, sometimes she was so indirect that it took the riders days to figure out what she was saying. They all enjoyed the challenge of untangling a tale Mrs. Reg had spun. But Mrs. Reg wasn't here to spin the tale. On the other hand, Carole was.

"There was a horse here once," Carole began, not having the faintest idea where she was going. Mrs. Reg almost always started her stories that way, though, and Carole trusted she'd get some inspiration. "He was a feisty one, that horse." Nice start, Carole told herself. May was feisty, too. Surely she'd be able to come up with something for May.

"He used to like to play in the pasture all the time." Carole could visualize this made-up pony, and she began to describe him for May. He was a bay with three white socks and a white blaze. His coat was a rich reddish-brown. He had a very smooth, supple walk, and he was the best jumper in the stable. That was a nice touch because May loved to jump horses.

Carole's story took on a life of its own. She added a mare who was the bay's best friend, and they would spend their summer days in the field, prancing and playing in the sunshine. And when little boys and girls wanted to ride them, the two of them just loved it. They liked being friends with the boys and girls best of all—much better than with the grown-ups at the stable. But then one day, the mare was sold and the bay became terribly lonely. He wouldn't eat the sweet grass in the field, and he lost a lot of weight. He even found he didn't like the children so much. Until one day a new horse came to the stable, and he became friends with the new horse.

Carole stopped her story there. She thought that was probably enough and that May would be comforted by the story as it stood. As it was with Mrs. Reg's stories, May was going to have to do a little thinking about what, exactly, the story meant.

May didn't have to do any thinking at all. She decided right away. She gave Carole a great big hug.

"Oh, Carole, I'm so sorry! But it's going to be better soon. Don't you worry."

She handed Carole the tissue she'd been using. She picked up her hard hat and thrust it on her head, snapping the strap efficiently.

"See you later!" she said. "And I want there to be a smile on your face next time, too!"

In an instant she was gone, leaving Carole alone with her thoughts. All of them revolved around what on earth May had made of the story she'd told. She'd obviously completely missed the point about how a new friend would come into her life. Somehow May had decided the story had to do with Carole, and she seemed to feel terribly sorry for Carole.

So much for trying to be Mrs. Reg. Instead of comforting May and giving her some understanding of what had happened between herself and Jessica, Carole's story had ended with May trying to comfort Carole. Carole scratched her head. The world didn't seem to be in working order at all.

On the other hand, something good had happened. May had been crying when Carole found her in the tack room. She'd been smiling by the time she'd left. It seemed that May had quite missed the point of Carole's story, but she hadn't been able to evade Carole's purpose—that being to cheer her up. Carole smiled to herself. Maybe it wasn't just exactly the way Mrs. Reg would have done it, but whatever it was she'd done, it had worked.

Carole made a mental note to herself to ask Mrs. Reg when she got back what she would have done. Then she changed her mind about it. She knew just what Mrs. Reg would do: She'd tell *Carole* a story about a horse at Pine Hollow, and then Carole would have to figure out what that was about. No, she decided, I'll just let this whole episode pass.

IT WAS TIME for Carole to get back to her charts. There, at least, she was confident. She could assign horses to riders, noting what she'd done, and everything would be right there in front of her. She headed for Mrs. Reg's office, hoping this job would give her more satisfaction and success than a few of her more recent tasks.

The young riders who were involved in the summer-camp program each had their horses assigned for the day. That took care of that. However, some of them came in only part-time, so their horses were now available for the noontime adult class. It took Carole a few minutes to sort out exactly what horses were available, and when she looked up from her chart, she found herself surrounded by six adult riders, all appearing to be none too patient.

"Can I get my horse now?" one woman asked testily.

"Of course," Carole said. She smiled diplomatically at the woman.

"I want the same one I rode last week," the woman said.

"And that was . . . ?" Carole asked.

"I can't remember its name, but it was brown," the woman informed Carole. This wasn't very informative, however, since ninety percent of the horses at the stable were one shade or another of brown. All she'd eliminated, really, were Pepper, a dappled gray who had been retired to the pasture; Delilah, the palomino; and Patch, the piebald.

"Bay or chestnut?" Carole asked, trying to narrow the field further.

"What's the difference?"

This wasn't going to be easy. Patiently Carole explained to the woman that bays were brown with black tails and manes. Chestnuts were solid shades of brown, often reddish, sometimes almost a golden color.

It took a few minutes, but they finally narrowed down the selection, and Carole assigned a horse to the woman. She *thought* it was the same horse the woman had ridden the week before, but she was quite confident that even if it wasn't, the woman would never know the difference.

"Next?"

"I want a different horse from the last one I rode in class," the next rider said. She smiled thinly at Carole, suggesting she didn't mean the smile at all. "I had a lot of trouble with him, and I don't want to spend the class time training *your* horse how to ride."

Carole didn't like the sound of this. All horses could be troublesome from time to time, but the Pine Hollow horses were really well trained. She knew from experience that when horses misbehaved, usually it was the rider's fault, not the horse's. Horses were naturally competitive, including competition with their riders. If a rider didn't establish who was in charge from the moment she got into the saddle, she was going to spend most of her time up there arguing with the horse about who was the boss. This woman who had wasted no time in establishing that she was going to be in charge of Carole's decision-making had apparently been unable to do the same with a horse.

"Who did you ride last time?" Carole asked.

"Barq," the woman answered.

That was a surprise. Barq was a really good horse. He could be a handul, but he certainly wasn't moody.

Carole started to wonder what the woman had done to get off on the wrong foot with Barq, but then realized that wasn't going to be productive. Her job was simply to give her a horse she would get along with.

"Now, don't give me some old nag," the woman said. "I had one of those once, and I spent the entire class kicking the old boy to get him to keep up with everybody else."

That would have been Pepper, Carole thought. Pepper didn't much like to be kicked. It would have made him go slower, too. This woman wasn't having any luck at all.

"So give me a horse with some spirit that I won't have trouble controlling. I've spoken with Max about my problems in this regard," the woman said. "I just don't intend to spend a lot of time riding at this stable if I can't get a decent mount. There *are* other stables around here, you know."

Carole didn't like the sound of this, and she didn't feel comfortable being on the spot. She and her friends were trying to help Max and Mrs. Reg. If she made a mistake here and cost Pine Hollow a rider, that would hardly be considered helpful.

"So what are you going to do?" the woman demanded.

Carole had no idea. "I think we can solve your problem," she said, stalling because she didn't know what she was going to do. What this woman wanted was a perfect horse that didn't require a perfect rider. She wanted a horse who was gentle and obedient, but who had spirit and was fun to ride. As far as Carole was concerned, that was a perfect description of only one horse—her own Starlight. It would mean she would miss a class, but she probably would have to do that anyway. Carole picked up the pencil, pleased with her solution to the problem. She was about to write in "Starlight" next to the woman's name, but she realized that wasn't a solution at all. For one thing, it was strictly against the rules to assign private horses to class riders—even her own horse. For another, it just wasn't right. All of the horses at Pine Hollow were good horses, and if she assigned Starlight to this woman, she'd be saying that wasn't so.

The woman cleared her throat impatiently.

"I think I have just the horse for you," Carole said, mentally running through all the horses on the list to figure out what horse she'd give to the woman. Then she saw the answer.

"His name is Patch. He's a piebald."

"Piebald? You mean like a pinto? A Western horse?" She said the words with disdain.

Carole could hardly believe her ears. Even the

greenest rider should be aware of the fact that the color or markings of a horse had absolutely nothing to do with the quality of a horse. It should be the last consideration when choosing a horse. This woman was definitely difficult! Then Carole found the solution.

"Did you know that Velvet's horse in *National Velvet* was a piebald?" Carole asked. "That's why she called him Pie."

"Really?" the woman asked. "The horse that won the race?" Carole nodded. The woman smiled then, and it seemed genuine. Carole had found the key. She wrote "Patch" next to the woman's name and made a note on Patch's section of the chart.

"Next?" Carole said.

The rest of the class turned out to be easier, and Carole was relieved. Assigning horses was a much bigger task than she'd ever thought. When the last of the lunchtime class was assigned, Carole sat back in Mrs. Reg's chair and put her feet on the desk. She deserved a little relaxation as a reward for her brilliant piece of diplomacy.

Her eyes lit on Mrs. Reg's infamous list. What more was there for the girls to do? Then Carole spotted Mr. Jarvis's name on the list. She looked at her watch. He was due at one o'clock, so that meant he'd be here any minute. Carole put her feet back down on the floor. She'd been telling herself all morning that she had to ask Max or Red just exactly what horse it was that Mr. Jarvis wanted. Now he'd be here in a minute, and she had no idea. Then she reminded herself that she'd just negotiated a very tricky settlement with a very fussy rider. If she could make that woman happy, she could surely make Mr. Jarvis happy.

A car pulled up. That had to be Mr. Jarvis. He was the only rider expected at this time. A few minutes later, Mr. Jarvis entered Mrs. Reg's office. He was surprised to see Carole at the desk.

"Mrs. Reg, you've shrunk!" he teased.

Carole immediately liked the man. She grinned and offered her hand. "I'm Carole Hanson," she said. "Mrs. Reg is away for a couple of days, and my friends and I are trying to replace her, though of course that's not an easy job. Anyway, you must be Mr. Jarvis. Mrs. Reg left us very specific instructions about you, sir, and said we had to have the right horse for you."

Carole was adopting the theory that the less sure she was about something, the more important it was to *sound* sure.

"Well then, she told you about me and Patch, didn't she?"

"Patch?"

"He's the only horse at Pine Hollow that I'll ever ride."

"Patch?"

This wasn't going well.

"She probably didn't tell you why, but it's an old story. I won't bore you with it—"

"Oh, I wouldn't be bored," Carole said, thinking that as long as the man was talking, she wouldn't have to tell him about the woman in the lunchtime class who was already riding Patch and who would now never give him up.

"It has to do with pintos," the man said. "The first horse I ever rode was a pinto, and I decided then that I always wanted to ride them. I know a horse's color has nothing to do with his quality"—and that put him a few steps above the woman who was now riding Patch—"but I'm very superstitious, and I simply can't be on anything but a pinto."

"Interesting," Carole said, though "interesting" wasn't what she was actually thinking. "Bad news" was more like it. She stalled.

"Also," the man went on, "I'm an artist. I paint with oils. It seems only right that a painter should ride painted ponies, don't you think?"

"Absolutely," Carole said. "It makes complete sense

to me." It didn't make any sense at all. By that same logic, since she was still in school, she should want to ride only horses who hadn't finished their schooling! Still Mr. Jarvis was apparently a good customer. Carole wanted to keep him happy. Then a thought occurred to her. Maybe, just maybe.

She scratched her head thoughtfully and considered the idea that had popped into her head. It was a Stevie Lake idea, if there ever had been one, and it was a gamble, but it seemed the only possibility. Carole wanted to please this nice, if slightly strange, man. Perhaps she could do it.

"I have to tell you that Patch is being ridden now," Carole said.

The man began to say something that Carole didn't think she wanted to hear, so she went on talking herself.

"Patch may be our only pinto, but he's not the only horse here that you will like. You go change into your riding clothes and wait for me by the door. Let me tack up another horse for you. I'll bring him to the good-luck horseshoe, and we'll meet you there."

"I only ride pintos!" the man said.

"I know," Carole said. "I know. And I think you'll find this one quite satisfactory."

Without further ado, she rose from the desk and

went to the stalls, sending Mr. Jarvis to the locker area.

Carole picked up some tack and went to the horse she'd assigned to Mr. Jarvis. "Piebald" was one of the English terms for black-and-white-patched horses, and "skewbald" horses had brown patches instead of black. In Spanish both of these were known as "pintos." Another English name for a pinto was "paint" or "painted horse." Now Pine Hollow had only one pinto, but as of the previous afternoon, they did have another painted horse. The colors weren't black and white—they were red and white.

"Hi there, Diablo," Carole said, patting him affectionately. She gave him a carrot, too, just to show that there were no hard feelings about the little chase they'd had in the field. He didn't seem to be harboring any grudges.

Carole inspected the paint job. She and Stevie and Lisa had been working at it quite unsuccessfully. It was going to take a lot of brushing to get it all out. Eventually the hairs would grow out and Diablo would be his same old dark brown, but for now, and for some time to come, he was decidedly brown, red, and white.

She tacked him up and led him to the door of the stable, where she found Mr. Jarvis waiting.

"I only—"

"It's a paint," she said, cutting off his words of protest. "I promise. And he's a terrific horse."

When she drew up to him, she made sure that she walked Diablo far enough into the sunlight for his very special red and white markings to be distinctly visible.

Mr. Jarvis looked. Then he looked again. He was about to speak, but he stopped himself. Carole held her tongue. That's just what Stevie would have done.

"Well, I never—" Mr. Jarvis said. But he wasn't angry, he was smiling. Then he laughed. "I guess if there's more than one way to skin a cat, there's got to be more than one way to paint a horse! All right. You win. I'll try this fellow. What's his name?"

"Diablo," Carole said. "He's a great horse, but be nice to him. He had kind of a rough day yesterday."

"At the beauty parlor?" Mr. Jarvis joked.

"Sort of," Carole conceded.

Mr. Jarvis took the reins from Carole and mounted Diablo. He brushed the good-luck horseshoe with his hand. He sat pensively in the saddle for a few minutes, trying to get the feel of the horse beneath him. He leaned forward and patted Diablo's neck. Then he turned to Carole.

"I noticed the new paint job on the front of the

stable as I came in," he said. "I told myself it was nice of you to paint the place just for me. I didn't realize at the time how true that was."

Carole saluted him in her best Marine Corps style. "We always try to please our customers, *sir*," she said.

"I can tell," he said. Then he signaled Diablo to head for the trails. Off they went, painter and painted pony together.

"IF ONE MORE person tells me that they want a gentle horse with some spirit, I think I'm going to scream," Carole said to her friends when they were all safely hidden in the hayloft above the stalls at Pine Hollow. They were having an impromptu Saddle Club meeting. They really needed one another.

"I can't tell you how awful it was to learn that only the man's *name* was French! He was as American as I am—as we all are—and he spoke pretty good French, too. Can you imagine? I thought he was the ambassador!" Lisa found herself reliving her profound embarrassment when she realized the mistake she and her friends had made.

"Do you think it was my fault?" Stevie asked defensively. "I mean, that's what Mrs. Reg's list said."

"I truly wish I could blame you for it," Lisa said. "But the fact is, I saw the list just like you did, and I drew exactly the same conclusion you did. We both got to thinking about Estelle and the Brazilian ambassador. No, I don't blame you."

Carole snapped the pop top of a can of soda and took a long drink. It tasted awfully good on the dusty warm afternoon. Lisa sipped at her apple juice. Stevie just stared blankly at the soda can in her hand. She was thinking hard.

"You know who we could really use at a time like this?" she asked.

Lisa nodded. "Sure, Mrs. Reg. She'd have a story for us about how some horses tried to band together when a friend of theirs left."

"No, maybe it would be about how Max—*her* Max—tried to fill in for the county doctor when he went on vacation," Stevie suggested.

"Or about how the farrier's wife learned to shoe horses just because her husband sprained his knee in the three-legged race at the church social and couldn't hold a horse's hoof between his knees long enough to shoe it," Carole said.

Lisa liked that one. She began laughing a little. It

was the first time she'd laughed all day, and it felt pretty good. Mrs. Reg's stories were always more than a little offbeat, and sometimes the girls suspected that they weren't based on the absolute truth. It didn't take away from their charm, because they knew that there was always something to learn from them. Right now it seemed that the one thing one of Mrs. Reg's stories could do for them would be to provide a good laugh.

Suddenly Lisa had a mental image of the farrier, complete with his leather apron, running a three-legged race. The image was absurd and it tickled her funny bone.

That was when Lisa's shoulders started shaking with laughter. Then while her friends watched, her giggles exploded, and they were positively infectious. Within a matter of seconds, Carole and Stevie joined in. None of it made any sense at all, and all of it seemed like the funniest thing that any one of the three of them had ever thought about. They laughed until the tears came, and then they laughed some more—until the tears rolled down their cheeks.

Each, in a corner of her heart and her mind, understood what was happening. The three of them had taken on an enormous amount of worry and work when they'd offered to do Mrs. Reg's job, and it seemed that everything they tried to do came out all wrong: a humongous paint job they couldn't possibly finish themselves, culminating in paint splattered on Diablo; saddling up ponies for six-foot-tall men; French lessons for an American rider; and at the bottom of it all, there was still no sign of Mrs. Reg's pin. The perfect antidote for such an exhausting and nerve-racking week was being together and acting silly.

Finally the laughter began to subside, but not the wonderful feeling of warmth and friendship it had brought. The girls understood, without saying anything among themselves, that the most valuable thing they had—more valuable even than a solid-gold pin with a diamond—was the love and friendship they had for one another.

"I just had a thought," Carole said when she could finally speak. Lisa and Stevie looked at her. "I was thinking about Mrs. Reg and what she would say if she could see us right now."

"That's easy," Stevie said.

Lisa painted a stern Mrs. Reg look on her face (although Mrs. Reg rarely looked stern), lowered her voice, and spoke the words for the absent woman, "What are you girls laughing about? Isn't there work to be done around here? You think this is some kind of game parlor?"

Since that was just about exactly what Mrs. Reg

would have said, all three girls began laughing again. But they didn't laugh as hard this time. The mention of Mrs. Reg reminded them what the underlying problem was. In the first place, they weren't doing her job very well. In the second place, but it was really the first place, they still hadn't found the pin.

"Oh, right," Stevie said, suddenly very sober.

"This was fun, but you know, I think we're really mess-ups," Lisa said. "I mean, every time I think about that poor Mr. French, I just can't believe what I did."

"*We* did, you mean," Stevie said generously. "But don't take it so hard, Lisa. After all, the guy thought it was funny, and he seemed to have a wonderful time. He *did* make an appointment to come back again next week."

"You're right," Lisa said. "But when he made the next appointment, he made me schedule it for Mr. English."

"See, he has a sense of humor," Carole said. "That's more than I can say for those basketball players."

"What are you saying?" Stevie asked. "They *loved* you."

"Sure, because they think I'm a complete ditz."

"Who cares?" Lisa asked. "I mean, I know they hurt your feelings, but you must have also impressed them. They pitched in and helped with the painting. We never would have finished if it hadn't been for them."

"I guess if it hadn't been for the painting, we never would have had a horse for Mr. Jarvis to ride, would we?" Carole said slowly.

"It seems that there's a pattern emerging here," Stevie said philosophically. She wasn't usually philosophical, so her friends listened carefully. "On the surface of it, we appear to be messing up totally, but when you look a little closer, it seems to be working for the best."

Lisa thought about that for a moment. Stevie was right, but she had the nagging feeling that doing things right in the first place was easier than messing up and then trying to find the silver lining to the cloud.

"You have a point," she finally conceded. "On the other hand, there's always tomorrow."

"Like what do you mean?" Carole asked.

"Well, we have until five o'clock tomorrow afternoon when Mrs. Reg is due back. Just think of all the things we could mess up before then. . . ."

"No, don't," Stevie countered. "Think of all the things we can make go right before then."

"Think of all the gold pins we can find before she gets back," Carole said.

Lisa looked at her watch. They had twenty-three and a half hours until Mrs. Reg's return. Considering what they'd done with the previous seventy-two hours, she wasn't very hopeful. She didn't share that thought with her friends. She didn't have to. The looks on their faces said they'd had the same thought all on their own.

ON FRIDAY MORNING Stevie sat at Mrs. Reg's desk and tugged at some of her hair. During these days when she and her friends had been trying to fill Mrs. Reg's shoes, Stevie had often found herself tugging at her hair. It didn't help much, but it was better than gritting her teeth. Her hair would grow back.

"But he *did* the wrong thing!" a very unpleasant voice whined at Stevie.

The voice belonged to none other than Veronica diAngelo, and the fact that it was unpleasant was nothing new. The fact that it was whining at her wasn't particularly new either, but the fact that she was supposed to do something about it *was* new, and Stevie didn't much like it.

The problem had to do with Garnet's grain ration. Most of the horses at Pine Hollow got the same feed for every meal all the time. Most horses had special diets some of the time, and a few had special diets all of the time. Pine Hollow could certainly manage that. There was a big chart in the feed shed, not far from the clipboard where Stevie had found the papers for the feed order, that showed who was supposed to eat what. Garnet had been put on a special diet. She was supposed to get a mixture of bran and whole oats in the morning for a week, while most of the other horses in the stable simply got crimped oats.

"There wasn't any bran in her feed this morning, and I could see that the oats in her bucket were crimped and not whole. Once again, Red has made a *terrible* mistake."

Red was standing next to Veronica. Right then his face was bright red with anger—even redder than his hair. He wasn't saying anything, though. He'd learned long ago not to argue with Veronica. She was just too dangerous. So it was up to Stevie to solve the problem.

It was a problem, too. Red *had* made a mistake. Veronica's horse wasn't supposed to get crimped oats because Veronica's father paid extra for her to have whole oats. Also, Judy Barker, the vet, had advised them to add the bran to Garnet's feed as a mild laxative because Veronica had been complaining that the horse had seemed sluggish. Garnet wasn't in any way *sick,* so Red's mistake was just that—a little goof—one that could easily be corrected with the horse's evening meal. However, Veronica seemed determined to make a federal case out of it.

"Judy *prescribed* this special diet for my horse, you know. It's not just that I think it would be nice for Garnet to get something special. It's been *prescribed* by a *doctor.*"

Stevie was fully aware of the fact that Judy was a doctor, and she didn't need Veronica to spit the words at her. In fact, she didn't think she needed Veronica at all. She wished she had the power to tell Veronica exactly what she was thinking, but she didn't. Veronica was a paying customer of Pine Hollow and deserved to get what she paid for.

Stevie looked at Red for help, but she could tell she wasn't going to get any. Red was holding his breath to keep from saying what was on his mind, and it wasn't an apology. Stevie thought Veronica deserved an apology. She also thought she deserved something else, and she suddenly had an idea of how she was going to deliver it to her.

"Well, Red," Stevie said finally. "It looks like we have made a little mistake here. . . ."

"*Little!*" Veronica sputtered, but Stevie continued talking before Veronica could start in again.

". . . and we're just going to have to make apologies and amends."

Those were the words Veronica was waiting to hear, and in her usual thoughtful and kind way, she told Stevie so.

"And just exactly how do you propose to do that?" she demanded.

Stevie pasted an angelic smile on her face. "Well, we're going to give Garnet the correct feed right now. Red?"

"Now?" he asked. "But Ste—"

"Now," Stevie said. She tried to sound authoritative without being bossy. It wasn't easy. She hoped she was managing it. Red didn't seem to think so. He tried again.

"I don't think—"

"We ought to correct this goof immediately," Stevie said calmly. "We wouldn't want Garnet to go without her bran and her whole oats, would we?"

"I could, but . . ."

"I know you're busy, Red," Stevie said sympathetically. "However, Veronica is right, and we just can't waste a second. We have to make it up to her. Right away."

Red got it. "You're absolutely right, Stevie. I'll get right on it."

"Thank you," Veronica said in a superior tone, "it's about time you took me seriously." She turned on her heel and stormed out of the office.

When they were pretty sure she was out of sight and earshot, Red offered his hand to Stevie for a high five. "I'm out of here," he said. "I've got work to do!"

Stevie grinned to herself. She'd accomplished something really good, and she felt good about it. Red was going to feed Garnet another full ration of grains, including the bran. The horse really didn't need the additional feeding, but it wouldn't harm him. It would, however, harm Veronica. There was no way she would be allowed to ride Garnet right after the horse had his ration of grain. It was a bad practice to ride a horse hard on a stomach filled with rich grains. So what Stevie had accomplished through the back door was something she never could have done in any direct way—she'd gotten Veronica out of jump class for the morning. It was just for an hour, but an hour without Veronica was a whole lot better than an hour with Veronica.

Satisfied with her own cleverness, she sat back in Mrs. Reg's chair, propped her feet on Mrs. Reg's desk, and grinned to herself.

"You look like the cat that ate the canary," Carole commented, walking into the office. She brushed Stevie's feet off the desk and laid out her new daily horse-assignment chart. "Tell me what's going on."

Stevie did. Carole loved it. She especially liked the part that a nice horse like Garnet would be getting a double treat—two rations of grain and the opportunity to miss a class with Veronica.

"Can't tell who's getting the better end of this deal, can we?" Carole asked.

Stevie was so proud of what she'd done that she wished there were more time to gloat. However, class was about to begin, and Mrs. Reg's office flooded with young riders, each clamoring for his or her favorite horse or pony. Carole was suddenly totally immersed in horse assignments.

"Oh, Stevie!" It was Lisa, calling from the front of the stable. Stevie was glad because that meant she had somebody else to tell about her victory over Veronica. It probably also meant that the delivery of hay and grain from Connor's was arriving. She grabbed the invoice from the last order just so she could check what was being delivered. She left the desk and the horse assignments to Carole and went to join her friend out in front of the stable.

"Stevie!" There was an urgency in Lisa's voice that

made Stevie quicken her step, though she wasn't really worried—because what could possibly ruin a morning in which she'd so totally outmaneuvered Veronica diAngelo?

When she stepped out the door of the stable, the answer to the question was right in front of her nose. It was an eighteen-wheel semi with large letters proclaiming it to be from Connor Hay & Grain.

The driver leaned out the window. "Where does Mrs. Reg want me to put all this stuff?" he asked.

"In the feed shed, like usual," Stevie said.

"This doesn't fit in the feed shed like usual," the man said. "This is a big order."

Stevie and Lisa looked at the truck. It was big. Really big. Stevie had seen deliveries from Connor's before. They usually just brought a few bags of grain and a couple hundred pounds of hay in the back of a pickup truck. They never brought it in a big truck like this—except for once when there was a three-day event at Pine Hollow and more than five times the usual number of horses were staying at the stable in temporary stalls.

Stevie tugged at her hair because as sure as Veronica diAngelo was going to have to stay out of jump class, Stevie knew that she'd done something wrong ordering the feed. But what?

Then a thought began forming in her mind. She hadn't looked at the date on the invoice before. She pulled the sheet of paper from her pocket and looked at it.

"Girls, why don't you go get Mrs. Reg so she can tell us what to do?" the driver asked. He was getting a little annoyed at Stevie, but not anywhere near as annoyed as Stevie was getting at herself.

There was the answer in black and white. The order she'd so happily duplicated had been placed exactly one week before the horse show at Pine Hollow. What she had sitting in the driveway was enough grain, hay, and straw to feed and bed hundreds of horses—not just the ones who lived at Pine Hollow, but ones from all over the county and then some.

It occurred to Stevie that perhaps the whole truckload wasn't for Pine Hollow. The stable had been doing business with Connor's for generations. Connor's certainly knew how much food they delivered regularly and that this "standing order" was intended to apply only to the annual horse show. Stevie felt silly having thought that the worst had happened.

"This whole truckload isn't for us, right?" Stevie asked confidently.

"Every bit of it," the man answered. "Just like you ordered. Now would you please go get Mrs. Reg?"

The worst had happened.

"I'll see what I can do," Stevie said weakly. She grabbed Lisa's sleeve and pulled her with her toward the office.

"What's going on?" Lisa asked.

It was hard to admit what a gigantic mistake she'd made, but Stevie explained it to Lisa, and when she did, Lisa groaned. "Oh, no."

"Oh, yes."

"But why don't you just tell them we don't need it?"

"I ordered it; I begged them for it," Stevie said.

"But we can't keep an order that size. There's no place to store it, and it will go bad."

Lisa was right about that. Fresh hay and grain were important. Horse feed that sat around was likely to become moldy, and moldy feed led to sick horses. She didn't have any idea what they were going to do, but the answer was not going to be to keep the whole order.

Stevie didn't even bother sitting at Mrs. Reg's desk. She just picked up the phone and dialed the number on the invoice.

She recognized the voice of the man she'd talked to earlier in the week. "Hi, I'm calling from Pine Hollow," she began.

"Oh, it's you," the man said. He sighed. Stevie wondered what that meant. "Listen, I'm glad you called. I got to ask you something really important."

Stevie was preparing herself to explain about her awful goof. She was so busy doing that in her mind that she almost missed what he was saying.

". . . Look, I'm sorry to ask you to do this, but there's an emergency over at the racetrack."

"What?" Stevie asked.

"I said, they had a fire in their grain shed at the racetrack. Everything is gone. The whole barn just blew up. And there's a meet going on. They've got a couple hundred horses over there, and they all need feed and grain. I'm asking all the stable owners around if they can cut back on their orders for right now so that we can supply the racetrack. I mean, if I don't get a truckload of feed over to them today . . . I know you need this order, but could you consider just taking partial delivery—for now? Please?" His words hung in the air. Stevie was stunned. She dropped into the chair at Mrs. Reg's desk, apparently completely unaware of the fact that she was sitting on Carole's lap.

"You mean, like you just want us to take a small portion of this gigantic delivery?" Stevie asked.

"If you possibly could," the man said. He sounded as

if he were pleading with her. In fact, it sounded like the kind of pleading Stevie had been about to do herself. It sounded more beautiful than a whole choir of angels!

This was the kind of situation Stevie liked best. It was a victory when she had absolutely no reason to expect one. It was as sweet as could be, and she was tempted to permit the poor man to beg some more. She couldn't do it, though. One reason she couldn't do it was that it wasn't fair to the man, who was just trying to do what was right for the horses at the racetrack. Another reason she couldn't do it was that she was about to start laughing, very hard.

"This is your lucky day," she said. "And mine, too."

"It is?"

"Yes," she assured the man. And then she explained. She told him about how she had just been guessing about what they needed, and when she'd found the old invoice, she hadn't even noticed that it was for the time they'd had the horse show. In fact, she explained, it seemed to her that there still was plenty of grain and hay in the feed shed, but since Mrs. Reg had wanted to have food by Friday, she thought they ought to take something. Could they have the amount they usually ordered—not for the horse show—and then could Connor's send the whole rest of the order to the racetrack?

"All the rest?" the man asked. "You sure you don't need it?"

"Every bit of it," Stevie said. "We don't even have a place to store it."

"You're right, this is my lucky day. I cleaned out my stores to fill your order because of all that funny stuff you said about Mrs. Reg and her sick friend—you know, the line about feeding her gruel. Now I find that when I'm in trouble, you guys come through for me just like Mrs. Reg does for her best friend."

"You want me to give you some gruel?" Stevie asked.

"No thanks," he said. "A truckload of grain and hay will do very nicely. Let me talk to the driver, okay?"

It was all settled in a matter of minutes. The driver and his assistant unloaded a very small portion of what was on the very big truck and headed for the racetrack with all the rest.

"Whew!" was all Stevie could say as she watched the truck drive away.

"Time for jump class," Carole reminded her.

"Ah, without Veronica," Stevie said. Maybe this day wasn't going to be so bad after all.

THREE O'CLOCK, FRIDAY. Normally Lisa was upset when it was three o'clock on Friday because on the summer schedule it meant that the week of riding was over and it was time for the weekend with no classes. Today she was sorry that the classes were finished, but she was really sorry that Mrs. Reg would be back in two hours and there was still no sign of her pin. The beautiful solid-gold, diamond-eyed horse was lost forever.

It was hard for Lisa to tell what upset her about it the most—the fact that she was responsible, the fact that the pin was valuable, or the fact that the pin had been a very special present to Mrs. Reg from her husband, who had died a long time ago. She'd thought about little else but the pin for days, and she hadn't been able to answer that question. What it came down to was that the pin was gone, and Mrs. Reg was going to be very sad, angry, and upset. Maybe there would even be some kind of punishment—like banning Lisa and her friends from riding at Pine Hollow. If that happened, Lisa couldn't blame Mrs. Reg in the least. She could only blame herself.

The riders walked their horses in a circle to cool them down, and as they passed Red, who stood by the edge of the ring, they pulled whips out of a bucket. One of them had a soda cap on the end, and the rider who got that whip was responsible for bringing cool drinks to everybody else while they untacked their horses. Carole got the soda whip. Lisa signaled to her that she'd be more than willing to untack Starlight while Carole took care of her task.

"Thanks, but let Stevie do it," Carole said, "You're going to want to spend some extra time on Diablo's grooming."

Lisa had forgotten. The advantage to riding Diablo was that when you were in the saddle, you couldn't see all the paint that was still on his rear. Lisa had been reminded of it, however, each time she'd passed Max in classes all day long, because he made an odd face every time he saw it. It looked like a grimace.

And if Max didn't like the paint on Diablo, Mrs. Reg was going to *hate* it.

Lisa was so despondent about the week's events that she barely noticed when Carole appeared at the door to Diablo's stable and perched a bottle of apple juice where Lisa could reach it.

"That stuff's really coming out, isn't it?" Carole asked, looking at the paint.

Lisa stopped her brushing and combing for a moment and looked at Diablo. The bay still looked more red and white than he ought to, but there was a fair amount of paint and paint-covered hair in the curry comb. Perhaps one day, in the not-too-distant future, the horse would once again be pure bay.

Lisa shrugged in answer to Carole's question. The fact that some of the paint was coming out didn't feel like much consolation.

"Look, as long as Stevie's taking care of Starlight for me, I'm going to run an errand for us," Carole said. "Dad told me he wouldn't get to the store to buy the food for our vegetable lasagna tonight, so I brought the recipe with me. I'll go over to the shopping center and get the stuff."

Lisa had completely forgotten about their dinner. She'd been so focused on Mrs. Reg's return and what *wasn't* going to get done by then that she hadn't re-

membered that there would be life after that. In fact
she couldn't believe Carole could think about anything but the missing pin.

"You're really going shopping?" Lisa asked.

"I know it seems odd," Carole said. "I was thinking
the same thing you're thinking now, but the fact is,
worrying doesn't change anything. It won't help us to
find the pin." It seemed like a wise philosophy. It
didn't change any facts, but it did change the way Lisa
felt about the facts.

"All right," she said. "You do the shopping, and
when Stevie and I are done, we'll try to find the pin
one more time. By then all the kids will be gone. We'll
go back to the locker area. I know we combed every
inch of it, but it's still the most logical place."

"Good idea," Carole said. "I'll cross my fingers for
you."

Lisa returned her attention to Diablo's coat. Carole
was right. The paint really *was* coming out.

HALF AN HOUR later Stevie and Lisa were once again
on their hands and knees in the locker area. Stevie
had found two flashlights, so the girls were peering
under everything they could, sweeping every inch of
the floor with beams of light, hoping to spot the glint
of gold, the sparkle of a diamond.

"Very interesting," Veronica diAngelo said.

Lisa jerked upward, knocking her head on the bench she'd been looking under. Stevie just grunted and kept on looking.

"It's just two blind mice now, and they aren't sweeping, cleaning, painting, or trying to do everything else under the sun to butter up the stable manager and her son, are they?"

There was a cruel edge to her voice, and Lisa didn't like it at all. It was sharper and more painful than the dull ache in her head where she'd bonked herself against the bench. She just stared at Veronica and waited for her to go on.

"So I've been asking myself, what is all this about? And now, with the two of you on your hands and knees at my feet, I think I know."

She couldn't possibly know, Lisa told herself.

"It's the pin," Veronica said. "When you called me at home, I began to think about it. I knew I'd seen it before and it wasn't Stevie's. It took me a while to remember, but a pretty piece of jewelry like that will stick in a girl's mind, even when she's been told that it's a fake. The only other time I saw that pin, Mrs. Reg was wearing it. It's not a fake. It's real gold, with a real diamond. And you lost it, didn't you?"

Lisa's jaw dropped. That was enough of an answer for Veronica. "Just as I thought," she said.

"You're the one who threw it at the cat!" Lisa blurted out.

"Me?" Veronica asked. "No way, dear. I never even had the thing in my hand. You just showed it to me, don't you remember?"

No, that wasn't the way Lisa remembered it. Not at all. But it didn't matter. Even the fact that Veronica probably *did* throw it at the cat didn't change the fact that Mrs. Reg had permitted Lisa to show the pin to her friends, and Lisa was responsible for whatever happened to it. Arguing with Veronica wasn't going to change that situation.

"Why don't you just go home and gloat?" Stevie asked.

"Oh, I wouldn't think of it," Veronica said. "Why would I want to go home and gloat when I can stay here and do the same thing? This way I get to watch the demise of Max's precious three favorite riders—the girls who have been trying to make themselves look so good all week just to make up for the fact that they've done something unforgivable. No, Stevie, I wouldn't leave here right now for the world! In fact, I think I'll just sit here on the bench for a while and watch the two of you sweat. I don't get many opportunities to do that. I'm not going to miss this one."

With that, Veronica settled herself on the bench and watched.

There was very little to watch, though, because even the most careful search of every square inch of the locker area revealed only a few dust bunnies. No horses, no gold, no diamonds.

CAROLE PUT THE two bags of groceries on the book-shelf next to Mrs. Reg's desk. She hadn't even greeted Lisa and Stevie, who were sitting in Mrs. Reg's office, because the two of them looked so glum that there didn't seem to be anything worth saying.

Instead she was greeted with a recapitulation of Stevie and Lisa's talk with Veronica. That made Carole feel just as cheerful as her friends. It even made her lose her appetite for vegetable lasagna.

"I think I know what I'm going to say to Mrs. Reg," Lisa said.

"You've thought up a way to explain the mess we've made?" Stevie asked.

"Well, I haven't figured out everything I'm going to say, but it's going to begin with the words 'I'm sorry.'"

"That sort of covers it, doesn't it?" Carole remarked. "Beginning, middle, and end."

"Very sorry," Stevie concurred.

A car pulled into the driveway at Pine Hollow. The girls couldn't even bring themselves to look. They knew what it was and who it was. Max had picked his mother up at the airport. That was Max and Mrs. Reg. Now it was official that they couldn't hide the fact that the pin was missing and they'd made nothing but dreadful mistakes ever since Mrs. Reg left, all in the name of trying to make up for the unforgivable.

"Oh, no," Lisa said. "I think I've forgotten my speech."

"It starts with 'I'm sorry,'" Stevie reminded her. "And if you forget, we'll say it for you."

They were quiet then, quiet enough to hear Mrs. Reg's exclamation from out front.

"Why, this is *beautiful*!"

"What's that, Mother?" Max asked.

"The front of the stable! You painted it!"

"I did?"

"Well, somebody did," Mrs. Reg said. "Who else would do it?"

"Oh, that's right. Stevie, Lisa, and Carole decided

to paint it. I don't know why—and they also took a turn at painting Diablo while they were at it!" He laughed.

Glumly Lisa thought it would probably be the last time he would laugh for a long time.

"Well, where are these girls who think they can replace me?" Mrs. Reg asked.

"I think they're waiting in your office," Max said.

The Saddle Club stood up to welcome Mrs. Reg respectfully. She almost ran into her office and gathered the girls in her arms for a big welcoming hug. It was not exactly what any one of them was expecting. They hugged her back.

"The front of the stable looks just great! When Morris sees how much better it looks, he's going to love doing the painting for our living room! Don't you think so, Max?"

Max looked a little confused and then seemed to remember something. "Definitely," he agreed.

"Whatever made you decide to take on that job?" Mrs. Reg asked.

"It was on your list," Stevie said. "It said to paint the front of the stable."

"No, it didn't," Mrs. Reg said. "Or maybe it did, but that wasn't what I meant."

"Did we mess up again?" Lisa asked.

"Again?" Mrs. Reg answered. "This wasn't a mess-up. This was a case of mind reading. See, my old friend Morris Halpern is coming tonight, and he's staying with us for the weekend. He is an artist, and he offered to do a painting of the stable for our home. I was planning to ask him to spruce the place up a little bit in his painting, but now I don't have to. He can make the painting look just like the place. Thanks!" Then she turned to her son. "Max, didn't you even look at that list?" she asked. "Did you just let these girls do absolutely *everything*?"

Max shrugged sheepishly. "They seemed to be doing a pretty good job of it," he said. "Actually, I came in here last night and took a look at the chart Carole made for assigning horses, and I was very impressed with it. You have to get her to show you how she did it. I think you'll want to use that chart, too. Can you show her, Carole?"

"Well, sure," Carole said. "But—"

"No buts," Mrs. Reg said. "Because if you've gotten as good at assigning horses as Max said, you may just end up with that job permanently."

"Oh, no thank you," Carole said quickly, her mind suddenly filled with images of frantic riders all demanding gentle but spirited horses at the same time.

"I'm sure Mrs. Reg does a much better job of it than I ever could."

Max smiled knowingly at her. Everyone appreciated that that was a tricky job. "Well, that may be true, Mother, but the fact is that these girls have been working some magic around here in your absence."

The Saddle Cub was more than a little surprised to hear Max say that. He'd been so busy since his mother departed that they had barely seen him, and they didn't think he'd noticed anything—except the paint on Diablo. He hadn't even noticed that the front of the stable had been painted!

There was a knock at Mrs. Reg's door then. Everybody turned to see that it was Veronica diAngelo.

"Can I speak to you and Mrs. Reg for a minute? In private?" she asked. Stevie, Lisa, and Carole knew what was coming. It was inevitable, and they didn't like it at all.

"Not right now," Max said, granting the girls an unexpected reprieve. "My mother just got back. Can it wait until morning?"

"It's important."

"A little later then," Max said. Then he turned to his mother. "And you should have heard what some of the other riders said about these three."

The Saddle Club was not eager to hear this. Carole thought of the basketball players and the ponies, then she thought of Mr. Jarvis and the painted horse. Lisa thought only of Mr. French, the non-French non-ambassador.

"My phone's been ringing off the hook," Max said.

Stevie wasn't surprised. Of course there had been complaints.

"We've got a whole basketball team that wants to learn to ride. Apparently their coach told them that horseback riding would help their balance. So four of them came and tried it. They loved it. I don't know what these three girls did, but the players just couldn't stop talking about how wonderful all the riders were at the place and how much they loved the horses that had been assigned to them."

Mrs. Reg beamed. Lisa was sure it was the last smile she'd see on her face for a long time once Veronica got a word in edgewise. "It's awfully nice to know that when I'm gone, my shoes can be filled by young riders Max and I have trained so well."

"I guess we did," Max said. "But I can't claim any credit for the French lesson that one of these young riders delivered. A new rider here said he never had more fun or learned more on a trail ride than he did with Lisa. He said something about having a friend who wants to learn Arabic and wondered if we had any Arabian horses. I don't know what he was talking about, but he signed up for six months' worth of trail riding. For that, I'll learn Urdu! I don't know what you did, Lisa, but thank you."

"It's a long story," Lisa said, stunned. "But you're welcome."

"Max—I need to talk to you *now*."

"Not now, Veronica." Max turned back to his mother. "Then there's the case of Mr. Jarvis. That man is quite strange, you know."

"Oh, right," Mrs. Reg said, remembering. "I never knew what to make of his passion for pintos. It's always been tricky having Patch available for him. When is he coming back? I have to make a note so Patch will be free."

"He'll be back, all right, but he doesn't have to ride Patch. Our friend Carole managed to convince him to try a bay. He says he enjoyed the experience so much, he wants to try to ride every horse in the stable. Can you imagine? Another magic trick from our young riders."

"I'm just thrilled," Mrs. Reg said. "I had a wonderful visit with my friend, you know—and she's much better now. She just needed some cheering up. Anyway, when I didn't hear from Max, I knew everything was going smoothly. Good work."

"I'm not done, Mother," Max said. "I also had a call today from the man at Connor's. You know how difficult he can be. Well, it turns out that Stevie here somehow managed to do him a gigantic favor, and he says he's going to give us a ten percent discount on our next order."

"Great! We'd better make it a big one, then, right?"

"Good idea," Stevie said, keeping a straight face. "And trust me, they're prepared for it to be big—very big."

"Good, but what were you doing ordering grain? I thought we—"

"Max, *now*."

"Just a minute, Veronica. Can't you see my mother hasn't even taken her coat off?"

She hadn't. In fact, Max and Mrs. Reg had been so busy going over all the wonderful things The Saddle Club had been doing in their own unique way that Mrs. Reg hadn't even sat down. Max put down his mother's suitcase and reached to help her off with her raincoat. And when her raincoat came off, the girls couldn't believe their eyes.

For there, fastened securely to Mrs. Reg's blue

blouse, was a solid gold pin of a horse with a diamond for an eye.

There was stunned silence. Even Veronica couldn't think of anything to say.

"Your pin—" Lisa uttered finally.

"I always wear it when I'm dressed up," Mrs. Reg said. "Though, of course, it doesn't belong in a stable. I mean, look what happened last time I had it here. You girls did a wonderful thing by calming Prancer. I had to rush after I picked up the pin where you left it for me in the locker area, so I never had a chance to tell you how proud I was of the job you were doing. But I'm sure Max remembered to tell you, didn't he?"

"Max?" Stevie said.

"You *did* remember, didn't you?" Mrs. Reg asked accusingly.

Max looked downright sheepish. That was enough of an answer.

"You mean he never told you that I got the pin?" Lisa shook her head.

"I certainly hope you weren't worried about it," Mrs. Reg said.

The girls looked at one another. Stevie shrugged for them all.

Mrs. Reg turned squarely to her son. "Max Regnery," she began. "Is it possible that you knew that these girls were worried sick about my pin and you didn't tell them, just because you knew they'd be trying to do everything in the world to find it and to try to make up for losing it?"

"Why, Mother!" he said. "How could you suggest such a thing?"

One of the things about having really close friends was that sometimes, without a word or look passing among them, they all had the same thought. At that instant three minds conceived of the idea that Mrs. Reg was going to have a few stories to tell her son about horses and riders who used to be at Pine Hollow. And there was a chance, just a chance, that one of them was going to be about a farrier in a three-legged race. . . .

The girls had to get out of Mrs. Reg's office before they started laughing uncontrollably.

"Veronica, what is it you wanted to say to us?" Max asked, now desperately trying to change the subject.

"Nothing," she said darkly, and then spun on her heels and marched out of the office.

The Saddle Club was close behind.

THREE VERY TIRED, but very relieved and very happy, girls piled into the back of Colonel Hanson's station wagon.

"Time for a Saddle Club meeting!" Stevie announced as soon as the door slammed.

"I can't believe it!" Lisa said. "We got away with *everything!*"

"We are something!" Carole agreed. "Never was there a threesome like us!"

"What is going on?" Colonel Hanson asked.

"Oh, Dad, you won't believe what just happened!"

"Probably not," he agreed, "but I've come to learn that when the three of you get together to try to solve a problem, it gets solved and stays solved, and even after it's long gone and done, people often can't figure out exactly what happened."

"That's a perfect description!" Stevie said.

The three of them started laughing all over again. It was a very different laughter from the sort of desperate giggles they'd all had the day before. Now they were laughing with relief and joy. Each felt the wonderful strength of their friendship that seemed to make The Saddle Club greater than the sum of its parts.

"This is all fine and good," Colonel Hanson said, interrupting their celebration. "But didn't I hear something about vegetable lasagna this morning at the breakfast table? I don't see any signs of grocery bags, and we don't want to go to the supermarket at this hour. What happened?"

"Oh, that's almost the best of all!" Carole said. "See, we were on our way out of Mrs. Reg's office when she spotted the grocery bags. I *did* do the shopping, Dad. Anyway, she said something like 'Max, you remembered!' It turns out that when she put 'Food for Friday' on her list, she didn't mean that we should order grain and hay, she meant that her friend, the one who is going to do the painting of Pine Hollow—and that's another story—is coming for dinner, and she wanted to be sure she had something to cook for him.

She was even thrilled that he'd included a recipe for vegetable lasagna. She's been meaning to try it for months!"

Even Colonel Hanson had to start laughing then. "There seems to be no end to the trouble you three can get into and out of at exactly the same time, and I have no end of admiration for this wacky skill you have. Still, I want to know, what are you girls going to make me for dinner?"

Carole patted her jeans pocket. She had the change from her grocery shopping, and she had the money Max had handed her to pay her back for the groceries. It was way too much money for the groceries, but it wasn't too much for what she had in mind.

"Simple, Dad. We're going to make reservations!"

Everybody agreed that it was a great idea. They had a victory to celebrate.

## A SPOOKY SIGHT . . .

A cloud swept across the sky, obscuring the big, round orange moon. Suddenly there was only darkness. All motion among the horses stopped as abruptly as it had started. After a moment of stillness, there was movement in the center of the herd of wild horses, where a silvery stallion ran in circles and whinnied loudly. There was something about him, something odd. Lisa squinted.

"Did you see that?" She couldn't believe what her eyes were telling her, but there appeared to be a white-clad figure on the stallion's back.

"It was a rider," Kate said breathlessly, sitting forward in her saddle for a clearer view of the now almost invisible herd.

"Don't be silly—" Carole said, dismissing the claim.

"Pure silvery white, just like the horse," Lisa said. . . .

# the
# Saddle Club

## Horse Trouble +
## Ghost Rider

Bonnie Bryant

RANDOM HOUSE AUSTRALIA

MUSIC SWELLED TO a crescendo, overwhelming the persistent flow of water. There was a flicker of light, barely perceptible through the cheap shower curtain. The bathroom door opened. And closed.

Swish! The shower curtain was thrust aside and in its stead appeared the long carving knife, which struck its target again and again. Dull, dark blood flowed mercilessly down the drain.

"IT'S ONLY CHOCOLATE syrup, Dad!" Carole Hanson reminded her father as she sat down in the chair next to his.

"That may be, but it's scary chocolate syrup," Colonel Hanson said to her. He hefted a handful of popcorn from the bowl and munched happily, his eyes glued to the television.

Carole and her father were deeply involved in one of their favorite activities: watching an old movie together. This time, since it was almost Halloween, their choice was the Alfred Hitchcock classic thriller, *Psycho*. Carole had read all about how the "murder" in the old black-and-white movie had been staged by dripping chocolate syrup, instead of blood, into the shower. But, knowing that didn't take away from the tension, even for Carole, who closed her eyes. Her father was right: It *was* scary chocolate syrup.

The phone rang.

Carole was so startled by the interruption that she jumped. Then she laughed and so did her father.

"It's got to be a wrong number," he said. "Nobody who knows us would consider calling when *Psycho* is on television."

The ringing continued. "I'll get it," Carole volunteered. "I can't see this part anyway. My eyes are shut too tightly."

Colonel Hanson barely seemed to notice Carole's departure. She picked up the phone in the kitchen and said, "Hello."

"Carole, we need your help!" a familiar voice greeted her over the phone. It took Carole a few seconds to recognize the voice of her friend, Kate Devine. Kate and her family ran a dude ranch in the Southwest, two thousand miles from the suburb of Washington, D.C., where Carole and her father lived. It was hard to imagine what help Carole could be expected to give from such a distance.

"Sure," Carole agreed. "What can I do?"

"Well, it mostly has to do with my mother," Kate began. She was talking very fast because she was very excited. And because Carole was being flooded with information, it took her a few minutes to get the drift of it all, but when she did, she was so excited that *she* began speaking very fast, too.

"You mean you want us to come out there?" she asked. "To help your mother give a party? Of course, it's for a good cause. . . ."

It turned out that Kate's mother, Phyllis, had volunteered to be in charge of a Halloween Fair for all the children of Two Mile Creek—the town where The Bar None Dude Ranch was located—and the money the party made was going to be used to help create an after-school program for the Native American children who went to the local reservation school.

"There was a great activity center there," Kate ex-

3

plained, "but it burned down over the summer. The kids don't have any place to go. They've had to cancel the whole program. The trouble is that Mom doesn't know the first thing about running something like that. Then when I told her how The Saddle Club had helped Stevie run her school fair, well, she just about insisted. . . ."

Carole smiled, remembering. The Saddle Club was made up of Carole and her best friends—Stevie Lake and Lisa Atwood—but it also had some out-of-town members. Kate and her friend Christine Lonetree were two of them. The club had two requirements: The members had to be horse crazy, and they had to be willing to help one another whenever they needed it. Sometimes the help had to do with horses and horse-back riding. Sometimes it had to do with schoolwork. Sometimes it even had to do with running school fairs. Now it appeared it was going to have to do with Halloween.

Stevie, Lisa, and Carole had visited the Devines' dude ranch several times. Kate's father, Frank, had been in the Marine Corps with Carole's father, and he was a pilot who occasionally flew a private plane. Whenever he came through Washington, he liked to combine the trip with a visit for his daughter and her friends. This time, Kate explained, her mom was planning to send him to pick up the girls.

"Wow. She *really* needs help, doesn't she?" Carole asked, now laughing at the thought that somebody as capable as Phyllis needed The Saddle Club to come to her aid. "You can count on us, you know."

"Oh, I know," Kate said. She paused, then added, "There's something else. . . . "

"What?" Carole asked, immediately feeling curious.

But Kate wasn't about to reveal anything. "I'll tell you about it when you get here," she replied.

Now Carole was even *more* curious, but she could tell that Kate was going to make her wait. She just had to find out what was going on, and that meant she was just going to have to convince her father, as well as Stevie's and Lisa's parents, to let them all go. They would have to miss three days of school; that would take some real convincing. Carole's mind raced. She'd found that spending time with Stevie meant she was learning to be a little bit devious, just as Stevie was. She had an idea.

"Hmm, school," Carole said. "I think your mother will be more convincing than I will be. Why don't we put her on the phone with my dad and let her do the work?"

"Great idea," Kate said. "I'll get her now."

"Hold it," said Carole. "On second thought, we'd better wait until *after* Dad finishes watching the movie that's on. I'll have him call back, okay?"

5

Kate understood. "I saw that *Psycho* is on television tonight. But it's not on until later here. If I'd known . . ."

Carole laughed. Her father was famous for his passion for old movies. "Don't worry. We'll call."

Carole finished her conversation with Kate and returned to the living room, where her father was gripping the arms of his chair as tightly as he had been when she'd left. She smiled to herself, even more certain that she'd done the right thing by not interrupting the movie. Idly Colonel Hanson passed the popcorn to his daughter, and they finished watching *Psycho* together.

As soon as it was over, however, she explained the situation.

"Three days of school?" her father said when she finished. "You'd need to miss three whole days?"

"But, Dad, it's for a good cause," Carole reminded him. She liked the sound of the phrase. It was true, and she felt it would be persuasive. "And remember, I have to do a certain number of hours of community service for school anyway. And, besides, one of those days is a teacher convention, so it's only two days that I would miss. Also, as you know, I've already finished my term project, due at the end of that week, and the class is bound to be spending a lot of time on that, so school would just be a waste of time for me anyway."

She paused to take a breath. "But if you are still worried about my missing the days, remember that we're studying immigration in the U.S. this year and the effect it's had on the land. You can't deny that what's happened to the Native Americans is related to that, so I'll have the chance to study the whole time I'm at The Bar None."

Colonel Hanson started laughing. "Very good," he said. "And when did you complete your study of persuasive rhetoric?"

"Huh?"

"I mean, you're doing a good job of presenting a solid argument with interesting facts to support your position. I'm impressed."

"Da-ad . . ."

As far as Carole was concerned, her father was the most terrific man in the world. They had always been close but had become even more so since the death of Carole's mother a few years before. They often joked and teased one another, and though Carole usually enjoyed it, she didn't think it was funny when something as important as three days off from school and a trip to The Bar None were at stake.

"I'll talk with Phyllis," Colonel Hanson said, sensing that this was what Carole really needed him to do.

It was all she could ask.

A few hours later it was all set, and Carole could barely believe her good luck. Neither could Stevie and Lisa. Somehow Phyllis Devine's call for help from The Saddle Club had struck a chord in everyone's parents, and they all had agreed. Each parent insisted on clearing it with the schools, but the girls were confident that if they kept repeating the sentence, "It's for a good cause," the schools would see the wisdom of letting the girls go.

"Isn't it wonderful?" Stevie squeaked into the phone.

"Fabulous!" Lisa agreed.

"Exciting," Carole added.

Stevie's family had signed up for a special telephone service that would let somebody talk to two people at once. The girls all agreed that it seemed custom-designed for telephone meetings of The Saddle Club. Her parents were beginning to think that the service had been custom-designed to make their telephone bill go through the ceiling, but as long as Stevie pitched in to pay for the phone bill, they didn't seem to mind.

"I've got zillions of ideas for a great Halloween party," Stevie said. "I mean, of course, we'll have a horror house, and then there should be a contest of some kind—like how about one where you guess the

8

number of candy corns in a jar—and then there can be a pumpkin-carving table. . . ."

"Can we have kids decorate cupcakes?" Lisa asked. She was quite artistic and always enjoyed making things.

"And we should definitely offer pony rides," Carole said. Although all three of the girls were horse crazy, Carole was the horse craziest. She had a way of bringing horses into everything she did. Her friends liked that about her.

"There should be a costume contest, too," Lisa said. "And a parade."

"Definitely a parade," Stevie agreed. "And we can lead it."

"What should we wear?" Lisa asked.

"You sound like Veronica diAngelo," Stevie said. "That's all she ever thinks about. Are you catching it from her?" Veronica was a snobbish rich girl who also rode at Pine Hollow. She was always more concerned about how she looked than how she rode. That was definitely *not* how Stevie, Lisa, and Carole thought about riding.

"I don't mean that we should go out West dressed as fashion plates," Lisa said. "I mean that if it's a Halloween party, we're going to need costumes. Frankly, I'm tired of being a ballerina every Halloween."

"Is that what you were?" Stevie said. "You're so lucky! The only costumes we ever have around this place are leftover pirate outfits from my brothers."

"And it seems like I'm always going as a noncommissioned officer," Carole lamented. Colonel Hanson seemed to have unlimited access to leftover Marine Corps uniforms.

"Come on, girls, we can do better than *this*," Lisa said.

"Hmmmm," Stevie said. It was a sign that her scheming mind was working. "Why don't we use Veronica as an inspiration?"

"Ugh," Carole said.

"And go as models? Dressed in designer clothes our parents can't afford?"

"No, that's not what I mean at all," said Stevie. "You know how Veronica is always accusing us of being goody-goodies for Max?" Max was the owner of Pine Hollow. Stevie, Lisa, and Carole always wanted to please him because that meant they were learning more about horses, but only Veronica would have called them goody-goodies. "You know how she even calls us the three blind mice?"

There was a brief silence while Lisa and Carole figured out what was on Stevie's mind.

"Great idea!" Lisa said. "All we'll need are some gray sweats."

"Hooded shirts that we can put ears on . . . ," Carole suggested.

"Whiskers!" Stevie added.

"Add sunglasses, a cane, and, *voilà*! There you have three blind mice."

"Stevie, you're brilliant," Lisa said.

"It was nothing," Stevie said. "Just the logical thing to do. Well, just the logical thing for a *genius* to do. . . ."

"And so modest," Lisa teased.

"I have to be careful, though," Stevie said. "I can't use up all of my genius tonight."

"Are you afraid you're about to run out?" Lisa asked.

"Not really. It's just that I'm going to need inspiration. See, my parents said *I* have to be the one to talk Miss Fenton into letting me out of school for three days next week."

Lisa and Carole laughed. If there was ever anybody who was an expert at talking a grown-up into letting her do something the grown-up really didn't think she ought to do, it was Stevie.

"I don't think there's any danger of your running out of genius for *that*," Carole said.

"Just tell her it's for a good cause," Lisa suggested.

". . . AND, MISS FENTON, it's for a good cause," Stevie found herself saying the next morning. She was standing in Miss Fenton's office, trying to sound sincere. She was sincere. She meant everything she had said, even the part about making up missed work before returning to school on Monday. She just wanted to be sure she sounded as sincere as she felt.

Miss Fenton cleared her throat. Stevie didn't think that was a good sign. "All right, now, Stephanie, let me see if I've got this straight."

The fact that Miss Fenton was calling her by her full name also wasn't a good sign. Nobody *ever* called her Stephanie unless there was trouble.

"You are promising to do all the work you miss *and* an extra report about the value of community service, so that you and your friends can take three days off from school to travel two thousand miles to give a party?"

"And it's for a good cause," Stevie added again.

Miss Fenton sighed. That was definitely not a good sign. "Well, the only thing I can say is that, considering what you've done at Fenton Hall in the name of good causes, I hope these poor people know what they're in for!"

It took Stevie a second to realize that she'd actually been given permission to go. "Oh, they do, Miss Fenton, they do!"

Then Miss Fenton laughed and shook Stevie's hand. "Good luck, Stevie," she said. "It sounds to me as if you've got an opportunity to make a special contribution to a worthy cause. I wouldn't think of standing in your way, and I can't wait to read your report. Next Monday morning."

The significance of the last sentence was not lost on Stevie. She smiled, nodded, and dashed out of Miss Fenton's office. She didn't want to wait around for Miss Fenton to have a change of heart!

Whenever the girls arrived at The Bar None, they got a warm greeting, but this one was particularly warm. The look on Phyllis Devine's face when The Saddle Club came into view was total relief.

"I thought you'd never get here!" she exclaimed, hugging all three girls at once.

The girls laughed. "You can count on us," Stevie promised. "Anytime. I mean anytime it's going to get me out of school for three days! Now here's what I've got planned."

Ideas poured out of Stevie the way water flowed over Niagara Falls. The girls hadn't even put their suitcases down before Stevie got to the horror house, which was going to be completely dark and *very* scary.

". . . and for that, we're going to have to peel some grapes—eyeballs, you know. Cold pasta makes great 'brains' in the dark, but I think we ought to use something other than spaghetti. What's that stuff that looks like brains? Radiatore or something? We'll have the kids screaming from here to Denver!"

"But won't they be scared?" Phyllis asked.

"That's the whole idea," Stevie assured her. "Of course, we'll make sure that it's all fun and they know it. We can't have everybody fainting all day long. Now about the crafts tables . . ."

Stevie and Phyllis sat down at the kitchen table and began plotting. As Stevie rattled off her ideas, Phyllis nodded enthusiastically and took notes.

"Where do these go?" *Thump.* The girls heard the sound of their suitcases hitting the floor and looked to see who had asked the question. It was a boy a little older than they were.

"This is John Brightstar," Kate said, introducing him to Stevie, Lisa, and Carole. "His father, Walter, is our new head wrangler." She thanked John for bringing the bags in and told him that the girls were staying in Bunkhouse One. Lisa offered to give him a hand carrying the suitcases over to the bunkhouse. John accepted her offer. Without a word the two of them picked up the suitcases and left the kitchen.

". . . and we're going to need to have at least one

really special prize. It's for the Kandy Korn Kounting Kontest," Stevie continued, as she and Phyllis picked up exactly where they'd left off.

Carole turned to Kate. "Okay, what's up?" she asked. "I mean, it's time for you to explain what you meant by 'There's something else.'"

Kate's face lit up. "It's really exciting," she said. "It's about a horse. Come on, I'll tell you all about him."

The look on Kate's face told Carole that this was a very special horse, and she couldn't wait to hear more. The two of them left the party schemers at the kitchen table and retreated to the lounge, where they could talk about something *really* important: horses.

"It's a stallion," Kate began. "He's pure white, and he's the most beautiful horse I've ever seen."

"Really white?" Carole asked. The only true white horses were albinos and were extremely rare. All the rest were called gray horses, no matter how white they appeared, because they all had some other colors mixed in with the white.

"A really white gray," Kate confirmed. "But it isn't even so much his color as his beauty."

Carole could visualize the horse, and she was thrilled for her friend. "When did you get him?" she asked.

"I didn't. That's the problem," Kate said. "He's in a

wild herd that roams on the federal land around here. I *want* to get him. I just don't know if I can."

"Isn't there a way to buy a wild horse?" Carole asked. "I remember reading something about it."

Kate nodded. "You don't buy them. You *adopt* them. It's a program run by the Bureau of Land Management." She pulled a booklet out of a pile on a coffee table. It was entitled *So You'd Like to Adopt a Wild Horse or Burro.* Carole flipped through it, and it sparked her memory. She had read about the Adopt-a-Horse-or-Burro program. If somebody wanted a horse, all he or she had to do was pay a small adoption fee and take good care of the horse for a year, at which time that person could own it. There were other rules, but it wasn't much more complicated than that. The only drawbacks were that the horses were most likely completely wild, and you might not get too much choice.

"The next adoption is coming up in another week, and I just keep thinking, what if somebody else adopts him before I do?" Kate said.

Carole looked at her friend and smiled. "This is almost funny, you know," she said. "You've been a national championship rider. You've been mounted on some of the finest horses in the country with bloodlines that would wow the queen of England. And now you've got your heart set on a no-account mustang?"

Kate nodded. "He's special," she said.

"Love at first sight?" Carole asked.

"Definitely," Kate said. "Just wait until you see him."

"How long do I have to wait? Can we go for a ride now?"

"I thought you'd never ask," Kate said. "Let's get Stevie and Lisa."

IT TOOK THE girls a very short time to change into their riding clothes and head for the barn to saddle up their horses. Each one had chosen a favorite horse on previous visits to The Bar None, so there was no delay in selecting their mounts for this ride. Kate had alerted Walter, and their horses were ready for them.

Carole greeted Berry, her strawberry roan, with a firm pat. Chocolate, Lisa's bay mare, nuzzled her neck.

"She remembers me!" Lisa cried, offering the horse a sugar lump.

"Possibly, but she may also be able to smell the sugar," Kate said wryly.

Lisa was just pleased to see "her" horse again.

Stevie rode a brown-and-white-patched pony whose name was Stewball. He had an offbeat look that matched his personality, which also matched Stevie's. This horse always seemed to know exactly what he wanted to do. Normally that was a troublesome characteristic in a horse. The odd part about Stewball was that what he wanted to do always seemed to be exactly what Stevie wanted to do. It was as if the two of them were made for each other. Back in Virginia, Stevie usually rode a blue-blooded Thoroughbred named Topside. Topside was an elegant, beautifully trained horse. He was almost the opposite of Stewball. Stevie loved them both for very different reasons. She gave Stewball a great big hug when she caught him in the paddock. He pretended not to notice, but Stevie was convinced he remembered her and was at least a little bit happy to see her again.

John was at the barn ready to help the girls saddle up their horses while his father rounded up Kate's horse from the field. When John offered to bring Lisa her saddle, she accepted. Western saddles were much heavier and more cumbersome than the English ones they used at Pine Hollow. Lisa was glad for the help—until John showed up carrying a pony saddle!

"Uh, John," Kate began.

It was then that Lisa noticed the twinkle in his eyes. "I just thought these fancy English rider types might prefer a little saddle to a real one," he said.

Stevie was the first one to laugh. She herself was quite a practical joker, and she always appreciated it when somebody thought up something funny to do.

"Thanks, but we can handle the real thing," Lisa

said. "And I guess I'm going to have to get it myself. . . ."

John smiled wryly. "No problem," he said. "I'll get it for you."

"John! What's going on?" Walter demanded, returning to the paddock with Kate's horse, an Appaloosa named Spot.

"We were just joking around, Walter," Kate said. "John's helping my friends saddle up."

"It doesn't look like he's being much help," Walter said. His sternness surprised Stevie, Lisa, and Carole. "It looks more like he's causing trouble."

"No trouble, Walter," Kate said. "It's just fun."

Walter grunted a response while he hitched Spot's lead rope to the corral fence. Then he fetched the Appaloosa's saddle and had him saddled up in what seemed like an instant.

"Wow," Carole said, admiring how quickly he'd done the job.

"Just trying to be helpful like I'm supposed to be," Walter said, holding Spot's reins so Kate could mount him.

John looked sheepishly at his father.

Kate climbed into the saddle and thanked Walter. It took only a few more minutes for Lisa, Stevie, and Carole to mount up, too. Then Walter and John helped them all adjust the cinches on the saddles, and they were off.

It was wonderful. Stevie, Lisa, and Carole loved riding in any form, and they particularly loved the kind of riding they did at Pine Hollow. But riding at The Bar None was unique. They weren't riding through fields and hilly woods. They were riding across Southwestern desert, passing tall cactus and scrubby bushes, around old rocky mountains, and along dusty trails. It was open, it was wild. Lisa found herself thinking that she had suddenly been dropped into an old Western movie. She could easily imagine cowboys and stage-coaches and one-street towns and half-expected John Wayne to pop up in front of her and drawl, "Howdy, pilgrim."

She smiled at her own thoughts and recognized that it felt great to be back at The Bar None, riding with Kate and her friends.

Kate's voice abruptly broke into Lisa's daydream. She was talking about the herd of wild horses and the one she wanted to adopt. Lisa listened with interest.

"The Bureau of Land Management has to keep down the wild-horse population," Kate was explaining. "If there are too many horses out there, two things will happen. First, the land won't support a large number, and some of them will die. Second, they'll eat everything that's growing, and the land will be even more barren. That's why the government likes to make the horses available to people who can give them good homes."

"It sounds like a great program," Carole said.

"It is," Kate confirmed. "Both the horses and the land benefit—to say nothing of us lucky ones who get the horses!"

"So when can we see your stallion?" Stevie asked.

"The herd has been collecting by the rise across the creek every afternoon recently," Kate replied. "We should find them there about now."

"Just show us the way," Stevie said. Then an odd look crossed her face. "On second thought, I don't think you have to. I have the feeling that Stewball knows exactly where to find them. He's in gear."

That was just like Stewball. Once he had an idea in his head, he was as stubborn as Stevie—and as likely to be right about it, too. All the riders decided to let Stewball take the lead. They trotted along a trail that followed a two-lane highway for a good distance, and then Stewball took a right and aimed for a mountain. He certainly seemed to know what he was doing, and when he rounded the base of the mountain and entered a small green valley where Two Mile Creek ran, they found that he was absolutely right. There, drinking lazily from the sparse stream, was a herd of about fifty wild horses. The girls drew their horses to a halt and watched.

It took Lisa's breath away. She knew about natural herds. She'd read about them. She'd even seen an educational special on them. But she'd never seen one. She'd seen hundreds, even thousands of horses in her life, but she'd never seen one that didn't belong to someone, hadn't been trained, coddled, shod, cared for. And here were fifty horses who didn't belong to anybody. There were no halters, no shoes, no feed boxes, no vets, no riders. These animals were wild. They didn't live in paddocks and stalls. They didn't eat processed grains and sugar lumps. They lived here. They lived everywhere. Lisa was stunned by the sight, and she wasn't alone in her thoughts.

"Oh." Stevie sighed. "They're beautiful."

"Where's the gray?" Carole whispered.

"Watch," Kate said.

The wind shifted then and carried their scent. Some of the mares lifted their heads and sniffed. They whinnied gently. Then the horses began moving around. The mares drank again. And then a pure white head rose, sniffed, and looked. The horse's ears twitched like antennae, reaching to pick up any sound. The girls were silent, but the horse found them anyway. The stallion called to his brood. At the instant of his call, all the horses in the herd were alert, awaiting his signal. Then, rising as if by magic, the pure white horse jumped and neighed loudly. And then the whole herd began to move, galloping off and away from the riders by the mountainside. The only sound in the desert was the thunder of hoofbeats, and then all that remained was the cloud of dust they left behind.

"Oh," Lisa said breathlessly.

"Just what I was going to say," Stevie agreed.

"YOU'VE JUST GOT to have him," Lisa said to Kate as they rode back toward The Bar None. "He's so beautiful. . . ."

"Did you notice the nick in his ear?" Kate asked. "It's very distinctive. It's like the imperfection that makes him absolutely perfect."

At first Lisa didn't think that was a very logical description, but as she thought about the horse, she came to think that Kate was right. Part of what made the stallion so beautiful was the wildness, and certainly the scar was a symbol of that, and would always be, even after Kate owned him and trained him.

Then, as if Carole had heard Lisa's thoughts, she

asked Kate, "Will you train him yourself? Do you know how to do it?"

"I know some things, of course," Kate said. "I mean, you can't spend as much time around horses as I have, or even as you have, without knowing a lot about training."

"Training a wild horse has got to be different from training a domestic one," Stevie reasoned. "I mean, that stallion has never stood still for a human in his life. It's hard to imagine that he ever will, either."

A smile crossed Kate's face, which told her friends that Stevie had put her finger on something very important to Kate: the stallion's very wildness.

"He will," Kate said. "I know it. Besides, Walter said he'd help me. He's had lots of experience with wild ponies. He knows what he's doing."

The mention of Walter reminded the girls of the awkward confrontation between him and John at the stable earlier.

"Is he always that serious?" Stevie asked. "He came down pretty hard on John."

Kate nodded. "I think Walter feels he has to prove himself. See, he's got some kind of odd reputation."

"You mean like he's dangerous?" Lisa asked.

"No way," said Kate. "But there's definitely something mysterious about his past."

"How do you know?" Stevie asked.

"We don't. That's what's mysterious," Kate explained. "Neither Walter nor John will talk about it at all, but it has something to do with John's mother. She's dead, I think. I overheard some parents talking about it at school, but as soon as they saw me, they stopped talking."

"Too bad they saw you," Stevie said. One of Stevie's favorite activities was overhearing conversations not intended for her. She was disappointed that Kate had been discovered.

"It didn't make any difference," Kate said. "From what I heard, it was clear they didn't know anything anyway. It's all just gossip. My parents don't listen to gossip, so they hired Walter, and nobody's sorry they did. He's a hard worker, and John works even harder. Sometimes I feel sorry for them because they work so hard and nothing ever seems to get better. Walter is always grim and determined. John? Well, he's nice and helpful, but he's hard to get to know."

"He seems lonely," Lisa said.

Stevie nodded. "That must be why he tried that practical joke. He just wanted to be friendly."

"That's what I thought," Lisa said.

Carole wrinkled her nose. "Well, it wasn't very funny. The saddle you put on a horse is very important. It needs to fit the horse, and it needs to fit the rider. I don't think it's something to joke about. I mean, if the saddle doesn't fit a horse, the horse can get sores, and they take a long time to heal—"

"Carole!" Stevie said, a little exasperated. "It was a joke."

Carole loved horses so much that it was harder for her to understand joking about them than it was for her friends. It was just like her to go off on a long speech about horse care and lore. Her friends took it as their responsibility to bring her back to reality.

"Definitely a joke," Kate assured her.

"And a slightly funny one," Lisa agreed. "It made me laugh."

"Well, Walter didn't laugh," Carole said.

"But he's *always* serious," Kate said.

"I wonder what secret he and John are keeping," mused Stevie. Her friends looked at her. There was nothing Stevie loved more than a mystery she could solve. There was nothing she hated more than not having her curiosity satisfied.

"Stevie!" Lisa said. "Some things just aren't any of our business. I mean, you have to respect other people's privacy."

"I suppose," Stevie conceded. "I'll mind my own business. I promise."

"Well," Kate said, "our business right now is to finish this ride and get back to the ranch. Christine's coming over later tonight, and Mom said something about wanting some help in the kitchen for dinner. Any volunteers?"

Three hands went up. Helping Phyllis cook was always a pleasure because the results were always so mouth watering, and, as they thought about it, it had been a long day for the travelers. Some good food would be very welcome. They headed home.

"IT'S A HEART!" Stevie declared.

"No, an oval—I mean an egg! A penny, uh, a saddle!" Carole suggested.

"A heart with some lumps around the edge—five lumps around the edge?" Stevie persisted.

Lisa shook her head violently. She scribbled some more and then looked to Kate for help.

"A treasure map?"

The girls were playing Pictionary. They were one team. The other team had been made up from other guests at The Bar None. The other guests were definitely winning, and Lisa didn't think her friends would ever recognize the turtle she was trying to draw. She drew a pattern on the turtle's back that looked pretty realistic to her.

"A bathtub!" Stevie was triumphant. But wrong. Lisa shook her head.

Now desperate, she tried drawing a hare to suggest a tortoise. That was no more successful.

29

"Time!" the other team announced.

"A turtle," Lisa said. Her friends looked at her scribbly sketch with a new point of view. "Three years of art lessons and I can't draw a recognizable turtle."

"Don't feel bad," Stevie told her. "Remember, I had trouble drawing a bell. This game is not about great art."

"Yes it is," a member of the opposing team chimed in—and then smiled gleefully. Considering all the very odd scribbles that had passed for pictures since the game started right after supper, everybody knew that was funny, and they all laughed.

The person who was drawing for the other team reached for a card, frowned as she looked at it, and then asked Lisa to time the round. Lisa automatically looked at her wrist. There was nothing there. It didn't make any difference in the game since they were actually using an egg timer, but it did make a difference to her wrist. She'd obviously taken her watch off sometime, and she had to try to remember where and when.

She flipped the egg timer and set her mind to work while the other team struggled with a drawing of a vegetable peeler.

*Pencil. Sword. Lollipop. I mean sucker—you know, the kind with a looped handle. Pot. Pan. Knife.*

Lisa remembered that she'd had it on when she and

her friends had been riding. She didn't remember whether she'd had it on when she was working in the kitchen and at dinner.

*Lasso. Lasso roping an egg. Lasso laying an egg.*

She recalled unsaddling Chocolate and noticing how much lather the horse had worked up. She'd given her a bath, and that must have been when she removed her watch. The memory came back then. She had taken her watch off and hooked it on a nail protruding from a wall in the barn. She didn't remember taking it off the nail, so it was almost certainly still there. It would probably still be there in the morning, but Lisa didn't want to take the chance.

*Toothbrush. Knife. Kitchen something. It's a—it's a— cheese grater? Whisk? Spatula? Rolling pin. No, not that. I mean—peeler. It's a vegetable peeler!*

Lisa had to smile at the way the other team all gave one another high fives for coming up with vegetable peeler. The sketches were unrecognizable to her, but it was enough to make it clear that they had won the match. Kate, Lisa, Stevie, and Carole all conceded good-naturedly and then politely refused the opportunity to get whupped again.

"Tomorrow we'll try Monopoly," Stevie said. Then she turned to her friends and whispered loudly, "I'm a shoe-in to pick up Boardwalk and Park Place, and we won't have to draw a *thing!*"

"Now wait a minute. Do you play 'Free Parking'?" asked one of their potential opponents.

As the members of the two teams cheerfully battled over the rules for playing Monopoly, Lisa slipped out of the room. She wanted to get out to the stable to find her watch.

She picked up a flashlight in the kitchen, slipped into a stable jacket, and walked out into the dark, cold desert night. Lisa pulled the warm collar up around her neck and stuck her hands into the oversized jacket pockets. She didn't need the flashlight as long as she was outdoors. The sky was clear and completely studded with stars. The moon, nearly full, shone down on her, engulfing the whole ranch in its silvery beams. She could see her own breath turn to steam.

The barn was completely dark, and since Lisa had no idea where the light switches were, she clicked the button on the flashlight and looked around her, trying to accustom her eyes to the shadowy darkness. She knew the barn well in daylight. In the dark it was totally unfamiliar, almost threatening.

Just because it's almost Halloween doesn't mean there are ghosts in the barn, she told herself. She almost believed it, too. She shivered and tried to orient herself so she could recall exactly where the nail was that she had used to park her wristwatch.

The stomp of a horse's foot on the wooden floor

made her jump. But then there was a whinny, and the sound was so familiar that Lisa found it strangely comforting.

"There, girl, there," came a human voice.

That startled Lisa even more. She'd thought she was alone.

"Who's there?" the voice called out quietly.

"It's me," Lisa said, and then realized that that wasn't much of an identifier. "Lisa. Lisa Atwood. Who are you? Where are you?"

"It's John. And I'm with the mare over here."

Lisa turned to the sound of his voice. She blinked in the darkness and then noticed a warm glow coming from the box stall at the end of the barn. She found John there, sitting on a stool in the stall. A mare, almost ready to foal, stood nearby, shifting from one side to the other uneasily.

"She seemed restless," he said. "I don't think she's ready yet, but she calmed down when I came in. I figured she just wanted company." There was a small lantern at his feet.

He reached up and casually patted the mare on her forehead. She nodded slowly.

"Sometimes they get that way," John went on. "It can't be easy having a great big foal in her womb, almost ready to be born, but not quite. Mothers have it tough, you know."

33

Lisa knew. She'd helped at the birth of a foal once. It had been one of the most exciting experiences of her life, and all during it she'd felt the anxiety and discomfort of the mare, who still seemed to bear it all willingly because there was no other choice. Lisa was also struck by the way John had expressed his concern—*mothers* have it tough. It made her recall Kate's suspicion that the rumors about John's father had to do with his mother. It wasn't any of her business. She pushed the thought back.

"Should your father know about this?" Lisa asked.

"Nah. He's sleeping. I'll take care of the mare tonight. He needs the rest. She needs the care." He patted the mare again. Then he looked quizzically at Lisa. "What are you doing here? Shouldn't you be getting into some hot game of charades or something?"

"Pictionary," she said. "We lost. I think I left my watch out here this afternoon. I put it on a nail somewhere, and I can't remember exactly where."

"Gold watch. White face. Black leather band?"

"Yes."

"Haven't seen it."

Lisa couldn't help herself. She laughed. John had a dry sense of humor that tickled her.

Slowly he stretched out his right leg and reached into the pocket. "Here it is," he said, handing her the watch. "I figured it was yours, and I figured you'd be

34

back out here in the morning. I didn't want to leave it hanging there by the hose all night long. Never can tell who might sneak in here just to see what the dudes have left hanging around. . . ."

"Thanks," Lisa said, slipping the watch back onto her wrist and buckling it. John stood up then and stepped out of the box stall. He closed the door softly behind him so as not to disturb the mare, who was now sleeping soundly. He stood near Lisa, and she found herself very aware of him. He was tall with sharp dark features. A shock of black hair hung straight over his eyes. His eyes seemed to see everything, and his gentle smile reassured Lisa. She felt as if she were the mare, being put at ease by this very interesting young man.

"It's a little spooky out here in the dark," Lisa said.

"Don't worry," John teased her. "I'll fend off any bats or gremlins who try to attack you or drink your blood."

"What a relief you're here," she teased him back.

"I'll also walk you back to the main house," John offered. Lisa was surprised to find that that was just what she'd been hoping he'd say.

"Did you girls have a nice ride this afternoon?" John asked as they headed back outside.

"Oh, yes," Lisa told him. "We went out and found the herd of wild horses—the ones that are going to be put up for adoption. You know about that?"

John nodded.

"Well, Kate has her heart set on the stallion. What a beauty he is—pure white, with this wonderful nick in his ear."

"No," John said abruptly.

"Sure, it's his right ear."

"No," he repeated. "She can't."

Lisa was startled by the sharpness of his voice. The gentle young man who was tending to the mare and escorting Lisa back to the house had suddenly disappeared. Lisa could feel his tenseness—almost anger. He halted and faced Lisa squarely. For a second she was almost afraid of him.

"What's the matter?" she asked.

"The stallion. She can't have him. You can't let her do it."

"Why not? What is going on here?" Then Lisa thought she knew what was going on. "Now, look. If you want that stallion, you've got every right, just the same as Kate, to try to adopt him yourself. All you have to do is register. I'm sure your father would do it for you because you have to be eighteen, but it doesn't cost much, and—"

"I don't want the stallion," John said. "And Kate can't have him, either. Don't you see?"

"No, I don't," Lisa said. "That's a beautiful horse. I

watched him protecting his mares, and I watched him gallop. He's going to make a fabulous saddle horse. Kate's going to love owning him, and imagine what it's been like for him to live in the wild—"

"It's where he belongs," John said. "It's where he's got to stay."

In her mind Lisa replayed the scene they'd come upon this afternoon: the stallion in the middle of his brood, king of all he surveyed, master of the mountains, ruler of the plains, untamed, unowned. Then she remembered what Kate had said about the very real possibility of the horses dying on their own.

"I know why they put horses up for adoption," John said, as if he were reading her mind. "It's a great program and it's well done. The problem isn't the program, it's the stallion with the nick in his ear. Kate can't have him. Nobody can. Just his rider . . ."

"I don't understand," Lisa said.

"Of course you don't. But don't let her do it."

"What—"

John spun on his heel and was gone, walking off in the darkness, returning to the barn, to the mare, to his own secret thoughts. Lisa was about as confused as she'd ever been. Who was this boy who felt the unease of a mare about to foal, kidded about saddles, picked up watches for safekeeping, walked young girls to safety in the dark, and had a mysterious notion about a stallion with a nick in his ear? What did it all mean?

A cold wind whipped through the moonlight and chilled Lisa to the bone. It was time to go back to the main house, alone.

LATER THAT NIGHT Christine Lonetree joined the girls in their bunkhouse for a Saddle Club meeting. This one looked more like a pajama party than a meeting, because that's exactly what it was.

All five of them were in warm nightclothes—mostly sweatpants and sweatshirts. It was October, and Bunkhouse One was heated only by a small potbellied stove and a fireplace. That didn't matter to the girls, though. They were too busy discussing plans to pay much attention to the occasional chatter of teeth. They also knew that the minute they climbed into their down sleeping bags, they'd be toasty warm. They just weren't ready to go to sleep yet. There were too many things to talk about.

"It's this incredible sort of dollhouse that my mother made," Christine said. She was trying to describe her mother's latest project. Mrs. Lonetree, in addition to teaching modern European and Russian history at the regional high school, was a potter. Sometimes she made what tourists thought were traditional Native American crafts. Most of the time, though, she did more original and creative work. She also worked with the children at the reservation's after-school program, when there was a program. Now Christine was telling them about an adobe dollhouse that Mrs. Lonetree had crafted.

"It's got two levels. Both of them are open so you can see what's inside, and it's a good thing, too, because she's completely filled it with traditional decorations. I mean blankets, wall hangings, even miniatures of the pots she sells to the tourists. It's incredible, and it's for you—for your party, I mean."

"It's going to be the big prize," Stevie said. "Kids will be lining up clear to the state line just to guess the number of candy corns in the jar. It's going to make zillions of dollars for the after-school program. Your mother is amazing—and wonderful. I can't wait to see it." Stevie reached for the bag of marshmallows, speared two with the long-handled fork, aimed the fork at the fire's embers, and carefully began turning them a perfect golden brown while the girls continued to chat about the Halloween Fair.

Once they had decided on several more activities— an archery game with pumpkins for targets, costume parade, and a makeup table—their thoughts naturally turned to the scarier aspects of the season. They turned off all the lights, lit a candle, and began to tell ghost stories.

Stevie was the hands-down winner in any ghost-story-telling competition. When her turn came, her four friends listened in total attention throughout. Finally she came to the conclusion of her story and lowered her voice to an almost inaudible hush. Lisa leaned forward, straining to catch every spellbinding word.

". . . and then a second rush of cold air swept through the castle and carried off Count Boscovich, Dante, and the raven. Miranda was alone in the castle, and all that remained to remind her of the horror she'd witnessed was the scratch on her face. And to this day, every time there is a full moon on Halloween, three drops of blood flow from Miranda's cheek. One is for her lover, one is for her father, and one is for the raven. It is the only proof she has that any one of them ever lived."

Suddenly a gust of cold air rushed through the cabin,

blowing out the candle. Lisa screamed. A second later footsteps approached and the bunkhouse door flew open. This time Lisa and Carole both screamed.

"Are you okay?" someone asked.

The ceiling light flipped on. It took a few seconds for the girls' eyes to adjust to the light, but when they could see again, they found that John Brightstar was standing there, and he looked very concerned. In fact he looked so solemn that it was all the girls could do to keep from giggling. Stevie actually couldn't restrain herself. Kate and Carole joined in.

Lisa could feel a blush of embarrassment rise on her cheeks. "We're fine," she began. "We were telling ghost stories," Stevie's very good at it, and she managed to scare me. Then when the candle went out, well, it just startled me." Suddenly it struck Lisa that it was very odd that John should just show up. Had he been passing by and heard her scream? She wanted to ask him what he was doing there, but he spoke again before she had the chance.

"You were telling ghost stories?" he said eagerly. "Great. I have a story I want to tell you." With that, he sat down on the floor, joining the circle the girls had formed around the fire. He cleared his throat and began.

Many years ago, so many my grandfather does not remember it, there were two tribes who lived and battled one another in these lands. They had warred for so long that nobody could remember when they had not warred. Neither could anyone remember why they warred. So deep were their hatred and fear that it was forbidden for members of one tribe to speak to members of the other.

One year, on the night of the first full moon after the harvest, a baby was born in each of these tribes. In the tribe to the north it was a girl, daughter of the chief. He named her Moon Glow, for the first natural beauty he saw after gazing at her face for the first time. In the tribe to the south it was a male child, son of a mighty warrior. His father named him White Eagle, after the great bird which had soared majestically above his home at the moment of his son's birth.

When Moon Glow was fifteen, she was betrothed to her father's bravest warrior. As a wedding gift, she chose to make him a cloak of pure white leather, embroidered with eagle feathers in the image of a bison—his totem. She traveled from her village to find the most perfect feathers for the cloak.

At that time, White Eagle was being prepared for the rigors of war. His elders had sent him out in the mountains with only his clothes, his knife, and a flint to make fire. He had to live alone and survive for half the life of the moon—

*two weeks—with only those tools. He could not see any-
body or talk to anybody until he had completed his test.
While others before him had died alone and in shame,
White Eagle was determined to survive. In the wilderness
he had made the weapons of survival—a bow and many
arrows, even a spear. He had eaten well, he had slept
warmly. He was sure he would survive his test.*

*White Eagle had been in the mountains for ten days. His
only companion was a white stallion who roamed the
mountains near his camp.*

Suddenly Lisa sat upright. John was talking about
Kate's horse, the stallion they'd seen earlier! She listened closely as he went on.

*The horse ran whenever White Eagle tried to touch him
or capture him, but he seemed to like being near White
Eagle. The brave knew that the horse was wild, now and
forever, and somehow the horse's very wildness was a comfort to him.*

*One day Moon Glow walked in the mountains alone,
hunting for an eagle from whom she could pluck feathers for
the cloak. She did not see the mountain lion who stalked
her, nor did she hear him. But the mountain lion saw her.
Without warning, he attacked, howling and shrieking in
victory as he landed on her back. Moon Glow screamed,
knowing it would do no good and hearing in response only
the slow, sad echo of her own voice.*

White Eagle heard the cry of the mountain lion and leapt up from his fire. Then he heard the cry of Moon Glow and he ran. He was only vaguely aware of the presence of the white stallion—a shadow at his side in his flight toward destiny.

When he found Moon Glow and the mountain lion, the girl was struggling bravely against the overpowering force of the wild creature. Without hesitation, White Eagle drew an arrow from his quiver, slipped it into his bow, drew it back, and let it fly. But he had drawn too quickly. The first arrow sped right past the lion and the girl and struck the ear of the white horse who watched from beyond. The horse flinched momentarily, but stood his ground bravely as the arrow passed right through his ear and landed harmlessly beyond him. Then White Eagle shot again, taking more careful aim. His arrow met its target. The mountain lion fell limp and dead. White Eagle ran to Moon Glow and took her up in his arms. She was almost unconscious and bleeding badly. White Eagle knew she was near death.

All thoughts of himself fled from his mind. He knew only that he must save this woman and the only way he could save her would be to return her to her people. He did not think of the consequences; he thought only of the woman who needed him. He began the long walk to the north, carrying the chieftain's dying daughter in his arms.

As he walked, White Eagle became aware that the wild white stallion walked with him. It surprised him because it was White Eagle's arrow that had wounded the stallion, but the ear showed no blood—just a nick that looked like an old wound, long healed. The stallion matched the brave step for step, never straying more than a few feet. And when a rock in the mountain caused White Eagle to stumble, the horse was there for White Eagle to lean on. It was the first time White Eagle had ever touched the horse. He was certain the horse would flee from his touch, but the stallion did not. He waited. Then White Eagle understood. The horse was offering to carry them to the north.

White Eagle lifted himself and Moon Glow onto the stallion's back. He cradled her in his arms as the sleek stallion made the journey.

It was an arduous journey, for Moon Glow had traveled far to search for feathers. When they arrived at her village, the chief took his daughter, but would not speak to White Eagle. The chief recognized him immediately as a son of the tribe of the south. White Eagle knew that his thanks was his life. He returned to the mountains.

Time passed. Moon Glow healed and White Eagle survived in the rest of his test. But neither could forget the other.

Then, one day, the stallion mysteriously appeared at White Eagle's village and seemed to invite White Eagle to ride on him. White Eagle climbed onto the horse's sleek back. The stallion took off immediately. Soon White Eagle found himself in the mountains once again. This time he was not alone. Moon Glow was waiting there for him. She was well and beautiful. At the moment they saw one another, they knew that they would love each other for eternity and that the stallion understood their love and had brought them together.

Many times after that, the stallion carried the lovers to one another. Moon Glow delayed her marriage by insisting that she finish the cloak she was making for her future husband. She sewed the feathers on the soft, white leather, but try as she did to make it the pattern of a bison, it was an eagle, soaring gracefully. Though she knew she was being disloyal to her father and to her tribe, Moon Glow loved the design she had crafted, as she loved the man it stood for. She would present the cloak to White Eagle, rather than to her future husband.

Finally the day came that Moon Glow and White Eagle had always dreaded. On the day that Moon Glow planned to give the finished cloak to White Eagle, Moon Glow's future husband trailed the white horse to the mountains. When he found the lovers together, the warrior was angry and jealous. Hatred for this enemy of his people filled his heart. Vowing that the pair would be punished, he seized them both, bound their hands, and made them walk back to the village in shame. There was no sign of the white stallion as they walked. There would be no rescue this time.

The chief was shocked to learn of his daughter's treason. He immediately condemned White Eagle to death and offered his daughter to any of his braves who would still have her.

"Oh, that's so sad," Stevie interrupted. "How could her father be so cruel!"

The others nodded as John continued.

*All hope was lost for the lovers. There was no escape for either, and to both death seemed preferable to separation. At the moment of White Eagle's execution, Moon Glow swallowed some poison. She lived long enough to watch the flames consume her beloved White Eagle and the flowing white cloak he wore to his death. As the smoke drifted up to the pale blue sky, she saw the distinct outline of a soaring eagle take flight. She gasped—whether in pain or surprise, nobody knows.*

*Then, at that moment, there was a thunder of hoof-beats. A pure white stallion came galloping through the village. He paused at the weak and dying Moon Glow. With her last ounce of energy, she reached upward, clutched the stallion's mane, and was swept up off the ground. Magically the horse rose in the air and flew sky-ward. Then, as the tribe watched, there appeared behind her on the horse, the pure white leather cloak she had so painstakingly made. On it was the perfect image of an eagle.*

"The lovers are gone now," John said. "Living together in eternity. But they say the horse still roams the wilderness, riderless, on an endless quest to help others whose love transcends hatred and bigotry. He carries the nick in his ear as a reminder of White Eagle's sacrifice, for the moment the brave performed the selfless act of saving Moon Glow, his fate was sealed. Our people call the horse after him—White Eagle."

Without another word, John rose and left the room.

"WHO WAS THAT boy?" Christine asked, sighing.

"John," Stevie said. "He works here. Wasn't that a *romantic* story!"

"Imagine—a flying horse!" agreed Carole.

"My mother has told me a story sort of like that," Christine said. "Only she didn't tell it as well as John does. You know how important the traditional tales are to Native Americans don't you? The generations learn from one another as stories are passed through the ages. We were telling stories long before the Europeans figured out how to write them down!"

"Well, that guy really knows how to make up a good tale and tell it just right," Stevie said. "That's the sort of thing you learn at your parents' knees."

"Jealous?" Carole teased.

"No. He's not as good as I am, but he is good. I mean, his story did make me shiver, but not the way my story scared you guys, right?"

"His wasn't supposed to be a scary story," Carole said.

"Oh, yes it was," said Lisa, speaking for the first time. "It was meant to scare Kate from adopting the stallion."

"I know. And it's not fair," Kate added.

All four girls looked at Kate, suddenly aware how much John's romantic tale had touched her.

"I want that horse. I don't know how he knows that I do, but he does. And now he's trying to make me change my mind. I just don't know why."

"Maybe he wants the stallion himself," Lisa suggested.

"But how did he know *I* wanted it?"

Lisa gulped uncomfortably. "I told him," she confessed. "See, he asked me about the ride we took, and I mentioned the stallion. He seemed all upset about it at the time, but he wouldn't tell me why. I asked him if he wanted the stallion himself, and he said that wasn't it. He just said that nobody could have the stallion with the nick in his ear. It was strange. One minute he was friendly and helpful. The next minute he was all strange about the horse."

A confused look crossed Christine's face. "Wait. I know him. Isn't that Walter Brightstar's son, John?"

"Yes," Kate told her.

"Oh, there's something odd about them, isn't there? I mean, I sort of remember some kind of rumor. . . ."

"They're really good with horses," Lisa said, suddenly wanting to defend John. "When I saw John, he was staying with a mare who is going to foal soon. He said she was restless and seemed to like his company. She did, too. She finally fell asleep while he was there."

All four of Lisa's friends looked at her. "When was this?" Stevie asked.

"After supper," Lisa explained. "I went back out to the barn to get my watch. John was there with the mare."

"Ah, a late-night meeting in the barn! Just *happened* to forget your watch?" Stevie teased.

"It wasn't exactly late night," Lisa said. "It was seven-thirty. And, yes, I did just happen to forget my watch. Give me a break!"

Stevie regarded her carefully and then shrugged her shoulders. "Well, you're *probably* telling the truth," she said. She was teasing and Lisa knew it. "But I think John was just being a practical joker. He's a pretty funny guy. I'll bet he just happened to be passing by the bunkhouse and heard my story, then couldn't resist the opportunity to join in on the Halloween fun so he made up that fantastic ghost story."

"I don't think he made it up," Christine said. "As I told you, my mother used to tell me one very much like it. The people around here know lots and lots of Native American tales. They're mythical and romantic. Sometimes they're pretty hard to understand."

"This one wasn't," Kate said. "At least John's reason for telling it wasn't hard to understand. It was carefully designed to make me change my mind about owning the stallion. And all I can say is that it won't work."

"Well, I'll tell you one thing," Carole said. "It may be a story, but it certainly isn't true. Remember that John began it by saying it all happened before his own grandfather's memory? That means it must have happened at least seventy years ago, and most horses die in their twenties, though a few live to thirty, maybe thirty-five. There is no way a horse is going to live as long as seventy years! Out of the question."

"It's a story, Carole!" Stevie said. "It wasn't meant to be taken literally. Besides, if the story is correct, the silvery stallion is some kind of ghost anyway. Ghosts don't have ages the way people or horses do. They just exist. Sort of."

"Oh, I suppose," Carole conceded. "I was just trying to make Kate feel better."

"Thanks, Carole," Kate said. "You did make me feel

better. You and Stevie reminded me that John's story is just a story, and I don't have to pay any attention to it. I'm going to get that horse at the adoption, and now I know what I'm going to name him."

"Yes?" Stevie asked expectantly.

"White Eagle, of course."

With that, Kate reached for a marshmallow and speared it with a long-handled fork. She held it over the flames in the fireplace. It marked the end of the discussion as far as she was concerned. In a show of agreement and support, her friends followed suit. Soon five marshmallows were toasting over the fire, and Christine took over the job of tale teller.

Later that night, cuddled into her down sleeping bag, Lisa thought about all the things that had happened that day and tried to make sense of them.

First, there was the stallion. She could still see him rising above his herd of mares. He was simply magnificent—wild and free. Lisa wondered if he would be any less magnificent with a saddle and rider on his back. Was he so beautiful because he was free? That was a silly idea, of course. All the horses who roamed the country were descended from domesticated ponies, who had originally been brought to this country by the Spaniards who first explored and settled these lands. A horse that was beautiful free would also be beautiful under saddle, especially if he was lucky enough to have a rider as good as Kate Devine to own and ride him.

Then there was John. And there was John's story. Lisa knew she needed to think about John's story, but first she just wanted to think about John. He wasn't like anybody she'd ever met before. She liked that about him. At the same time, it frightened her a little bit. He was handsome, to be sure, but that wasn't what frightened her. He seemed like at least two different boys at once. He was the kind, gentle, caring young man who sat with a mare for hours, watching and comforting her when his own father should have been doing it. That gave Lisa a start. Just where had Walter been while all this was going on? He *should* have been the one with the mare. Was John covering for him? Lisa decided not to think about that right then, either.

Then there was the other John. That was the mysterious John who wasn't going to tell why Kate shouldn't adopt the stallion. That same John was the one who had shown up at the bunkhouse, walked in uninvited (it was a good thing they were all wearing sweatpants and sweatshirts to sleep in!), told a confusing and probably untrue story clearly designed to make Kate change her mind about owning the stallion, and then just walked out. What was he trying to do? More important, why was he trying to do it?

Lisa's mind replayed her conversations with John,

especially the story he'd told. In her mind she heard it over and over again. Finally she fell asleep with the image of the horse rising into the sky above the village, carrying the star-crossed lovers to their destiny. The image was to remain with her for a very long time.

6

"IF ONE MORE person asks me if they're going to have to peel the grapes, I'll scream," Stevie announced.

Lisa laughed. Stevie was pretending to be angry, but the fact was she was in her element. All five of the girls were at the regional high school, where the basement had been turned over to them for the party that was to take place tomorrow. Students from the school wandered in and out during their free periods, offering to help decorate or otherwise get ready. Kate and Christine had special dispensation from their own schools to have the time off to put together the Halloween Fair—as long as they got their homework in on time and got the notes they missed from classmates.

"Don't worry about your homework," Stevie told

them. "That's one of the things The Saddle Club is the very best at."

"You mean you're going to do it for me?" Kate asked, teasing.

"No, not me," Stevie assured her. "If I did it, you'd both flunk out. No, the one who does the best homework is Lisa. She can do anything!"

"Ahem," Lisa said. "She can also follow instructions. Like I'll be glad to help anybody with their homework. I don't *do* other people's work."

"Whatever," said Stevie. "Just don't worry. We'll come through for you."

"You always have," Christine said. "And that's what you're doing now, right?"

Stevie looked down. She was standing on top of a very tall ladder. "Actually," she said, "at this moment I'm not so sure." In one hand she had some orange crepe paper, and in the other was a piece of tape. The problem was she was going to have to put the two of them together on a spot she could reach. The best she could do was the edge of a fluorescent lamp.

"Okay?" she asked. Lisa was standing on the floor, holding the ladder to steady it.

"Sort of," Lisa told her. "But you'd better hurry down now. Two more people want to know who's going to peel the grapes."

"Yeooooooo!" Stevie said. But she was laughing

when she got back down to ground level. "I think I've got an idea," she said to Lisa, her eyes sparkling. That was usually a sign of a really good or a really bad idea. With Stevie it was sometimes hard to tell which was which. "The next person who asks me about the grapes will be assigned the job of putting up the rest of the crepe paper."

John Brightstar sauntered into the basement. "Hey, good morning, girls!" he greeted them. "The ninth grade has a free period, and my teacher said I should offer to help. Any grapes need peeling?"

Stevie blinked in astonishment. "No," she said sweetly. "But we have another job that's right up your alley. Come on aboard."

It turned out that John was actually the perfect person for the job of hanging orange and black crepe paper, because he was tall enough to reach the ceiling from the top of the ladder. It also meant that Lisa was assigned to retain her position of holding the ladder and steadying it. She held on very tightly.

Stevie didn't waste a second. There was an awful lot of work to do and it didn't seem as if there were anywhere near enough time to do it. Stevie mustered her troops to the area she'd designated as the horror house and began partitioning it off.

One section was where the awful things to feel—including the peeled grapes that blindfolded visitors

59

would be told were eyeballs—would be laid out. Stevie knew that peeling grapes was a boring job, but she thought she and the girls could do it that night in the kitchen at The Bar None. After all, they'd just need a few of them. What was the big deal? They'd also cook the pasta designated as brains and fill long oiled balloons with water and tell everyone they were entrails. Stevie was pretty sure they could think of some more disgusting things before the fair, too. She just had to put her mind to it.

"Okay, this is where we're going to have the wind tunnel. Can anybody get their hands on a tube-type vacuum cleaner so we can reverse the air flow?"

Two hands went up. That solved that problem. It also gave Stevie two volunteers to run their own mothers' vacuum cleaners, since Stevie was pretty sure the mothers would insist on it anyway.

"And next comes the ghost mirror," Stevie said. "Is there a full-length mirror we can paint stuff on?"

There was. One of the high school students "borrowed" it from the girls' room upstairs, and Stevie assigned an aspiring art student the job of painting a suggestive ghost on it. That way, the "guest" in the horror house would see herself or himself, *plus* a ghost. Anyone who pooh-poohed the ghost would be treated to the immediate appearance of somebody dressed in an identical outfit.

"It's going to be great!" Stevie said. "Just make sure the ghost you paint is just a little wispy. We don't want anybody to be able to see anything clearly. The kids' imaginations are going to be doing an awful lot of work."

"Got it!" the artist said, and then disappeared to "borrow" some paints from the art room.

"Next, we have to have something for the kids to fall down on that won't hurt them."

"Mattresses?" somebody suggested.

"Probably," Stevie said. "But I'm open to other suggestions."

"Rubber balls? We've got a ton of them in the gym."

"We'd really need a ton of them," Stevie said. "I mean, this has to be safe. In spite of what the kids think, we have to treat them like precious packages. We want them scared, not hurt."

"You mean precious packages, like fragile things you ship places?" a redheaded boy asked. Stevie had the feeling he was on to something.

"Yes, very fragile," Stevie agreed. "What's on your mind?"

"Well, my father runs this mail-order business, and he just got a truckload—and I mean truckload—of Styrofoam peanuts. He uses them all right, but he doesn't use that many, and it's a three-year supply. The place that delivered them doesn't want to take them back. You getting the picture?"

"Perfect!" Stevie declared. "I'm sure he can get a tax deduction for a donation to a worthy cause. . . ."

"Probably, but I think he'll be happy enough just to get them out of the backyard. My mom won't mind, either."

"I hereby declare you in charge," Stevie said. "And we'll set that up over here. . . ."

There was so much to do, and it was all so much fun, that the girls barely noticed as the hours passed. By midafternoon, it seemed that Stevie had everybody in town—and certainly everybody in the school— jumping at her commands. Phyllis Devine pitched in and beamed proudly to see how well her team— The Saddle Club—was running the fair she was in charge of.

"Phyllis, you're brilliant," the principal of the school said, admiring how well everybody was working together. "I can't get these kids to work like this to put on a dance for themselves, much less to put together a Halloween Fair for little ones. What's your secret?" he asked.

"My magic ingredient?" She shrugged. "Hard to explain, but it all has to do with horses."

Since there wasn't a horse in sight (Carole was working on the pony rides *outside* the school), the principal couldn't make any sense out of Phyllis's remark. It didn't get any clearer when Stevie, Lisa,

Kate, and Christine all started laughing, either. The confused principal returned to his office, where he could fill out some more forms.

By four o'clock it was time to call it a day. They could finish up everything the following morning before the fair actually began. Surveying the work they'd done, though, they could hardly believe they'd only begun that morning. In a mere six or seven hours they'd taken a perfectly normal school basement and rec room and turned it into a total disaster area. Crepe paper hung from every possible place, curtains had been set up to divide the horror house into its components, including a hiding place for the reverse vacuumers and a ramp that would lead to the sea of Styrofoam, and tables had been strewn everywhere. Only Stevie knew which activity would be on which table. For now it just looked like a mess.

Stevie put her hands on her hips and admired the room filled with half-finished projects. "Isn't it just beautiful?" she asked. Only good friends would agree. They did.

"Okay, so what's next?" Lisa asked. She stifled a yawn. She was tired from holding the ladder all afternoon.

"Next is costumes," Stevie said.

"Wait a minute, we know what we're going to be," Carole reminded her. "We're going to be mice."

"Sure, but that doesn't mean there isn't any work to do. We have to figure out how to make ears and check that we've got the makeup we need for our whiskers. There's a lot left to do. We can't waste a minute."

"My mother promised me she'd help me with my costume tonight," Christine said. "I'll bet she can make six mouse ears in no time at all. Why don't you come to my house?"

"Can she do a farmer's wife?" Kate asked, suddenly inspired. After all, if her best friends were going to be the three blind mice, the least she could do was join them.

"In a New York minute," Christine promised. "Actually, I think she's got a gingham dress and an apron already. She might have to take the dress in a little, or else stuff it—oh, come on home with me and let's see what she can do. In any case, you all will have a chance to see the adobe dollhouse."

"Great," Stevie said. "I'm really dying to see it."

It took the girls a few minutes to tidy up a few (very few) things so they would know where to begin the next day. Stevie, Lisa, and Carole had each brought their basic mouse outfits—gray sweatpants and hooded sweatshirts—assuming that they'd end up at the store in town to look for something to make ears from. The fact that Mrs. Lonetree might be able to help them was awfully good news. She was a very creative person and probably would make better mouse ears than they could ever hope to!

The best news, though, was that getting there was going to be half the fun. The girls had ridden their horses into town that morning and had let them loose in a corral the high school maintained for the students who rode to school. Now they would ride to Christine's house and eventually back to The Bar None. That was always a pleasant prospect, but now all the more so since it was quite dark outside.

Stevie gave a final tug to the cinch on Stewball's saddle and climbed aboard. "It's a good thing horses can see in the dark," she said. "Because I don't think I can see a thing."

"Don't be so sure," Christine told her. "Once your eyes adjust to the darkness, you'll be surprised how much you can see—especially since there are a lot of stars out tonight."

"And the moon?" Lisa asked, looking to the sky.

"It's not up yet," Christine said. "But when it comes out, it should be nice, because it's almost full. I love riding by moonlight."

"Me, too," Carole said. She climbed into the saddle. "Actually, that's an understatement," she continued. "The fact is that I love riding anywhere, anytime. That includes by moonlight."

"Me, too," Kate said. Then she asked, "Everybody ready?"

They were, and they were off. Christine led the way since she knew the route to her own house the best. At first the girls followed the road out of town. They knew that they could take the road all the way to the Lonetrees' house, but the fact was that it was going to be a lot more fun to leave the roadway and cut across the open land. Their journey was aided then by the fact that the moon rose at the moment they left the road. It stood on the horizon, nearly full, big, orange, and bright. It almost seemed to lay a path for them to follow.

"This way," Christine said. It was easy to see where they were going. It was a fun ride.

Even though each girl was quite aware of the fact that they were in the twentieth century, not far from things like power plants and gas stations and a school with no fewer than two computer labs, it somehow seemed to each of them as if they had left all that behind. Every step into the open countryside felt like a step back in time, away from electronics and nuclear power, away from microwaves and dishwashers. The years dropped off as a snake sheds its skin. Lisa found herself thinking about life in the Old West, wondering what it would have been like just to survive. Stevie's mind turned to images of cowboys and stagecoaches, just as she'd seen in so many movies. Carole found herself thinking about the animals that had once wandered so freely and so safely on the land. Christine thought of her own family's people, part of the original American West. Kate thought about the horses, brought here from Europe, allowed to roam free—the magnificent animals who ruled the prairies and the desert lands.

*How-oooooooo!*

Even though the girls from Virginia had never heard that sound before, they knew instantly what it was. It was unmistakable. It was a coyote.

"Watch it!" Christine warned.

The girls all drew their horses to a halt. They listened again. The coyote howled again.

*How-oooooooo!*

He was a good distance from them, so they knew they weren't in any immediate danger, but the fact that there was one coyote around could mean that there were more. Coyotes didn't usually attack humans. Still, they were dangerous animals, and it made sense for the girls to hurry on their way.

"Okay, let's go," Christine said.

"No, wait!" Kate said, staying still. "Look!"

The girls looked where she pointed. The object of the coyote's call became apparent then, as a cloud of dust rose from the dry earth to the south of where they waited.

"It's the herd," Carole said. "The horses! They must have been startled by the coyote. Look at them."

While the motionless horses had been nearly invisible to the girls' eyes, the moving herd was very apparent. The mares and their young were milling frantically and simply making their presence more apparent to all the creatures around, especially the coyotes.

"We've got to help them!" Carole said.

"By doing what?" Christine asked. "What's going on here is what's been going on for thousands of years. There's nothing for us to do."

"But the coyotes—they could attack the horses!" Carole couldn't bear the idea that one of the herd might serve as dinner for the coyotes.

"The horses can take care of themselves," Kate said. Her eyes didn't move from the scene in front of her.

Her friends watched as well. Then the entire scene was dimmed when a cloud swept across the sky, obscuring the big, round orange moon. Suddenly there was only darkness.

*How-ooooooo!*

All motion among the horses stopped as abruptly as it had started. After a moment of stillness, there was movement in the center of the pack, where a silvery stallion ran in circles and whinnied loudly. There

68

was something else about him, something odd. Lisa squinted.

"Did you see that?" She couldn't believe what her eyes were telling her, but there appeared to be a white-clad figure on the stallion's back.

"What was it?"

The horse shifted directions again and began a gallop to safety. Unquestioning, the brood followed his lead. Within seconds the whole herd began to disappear behind an outcrop of rocks.

"It was a rider," Kate said breathlessly, sitting forward in her saddle for a clearer view of the now almost invisible herd.

"Don't be silly—" Carole said, dismissing the claim.

"Pure silvery white, just like the horse," Lisa said.

"And just like White Eagle—" Christine added.

"Oh, come on you guys," Stevie said. "It's just John, playing another joke on us."

"Do you think—?" Kate began.

"Of course I do," Stevie said. "You don't really believe in ghosts, do you?"

Kate closed her eyes and shook her head as if trying to shake the image from her mind. Then she opened her eyes again. "I don't suppose so," she said. "You're probably right, it was John."

"Well, more power to him," Carole said. "At least

he figured out how to save the horses from being attacked by the coyotes."

"I don't think that was what he had in mind when he planned the joke," Kate said. "I think he was just trying to scare me away again."

"I don't think we're going to get anywhere trying to know what's going on in John Brightstar's mind," Christine said. "Let's just get to my house."

The girls proceeded together. The thoughts of pioneer days were gone now for Lisa. The only thing on her mind was John. Maybe Kate was right—he was trying to scare her off—but Lisa had to admit that that was a pretty incredible thing to do. Not only was he the kind of boy who would take care of an ailing horse and come up with a deliciously romantic tale to justify keeping a horse in the wild, he'd even risk riding the creature!

Or was it possible, just possible, that John's story was true and the stallion had come to help them because they were helping the children on the Indian reservation?

Lisa really didn't know what to think. All she knew was that she had a lot to think about. And his name was John.

MRS. LONETREE WAS positively a whiz with her sewing machine. Within what seemed like a matter of minutes, she'd created three adorable sets of mouse ears—field mice, not Mickey—and had them tacked onto the girls' sweatshirt hoods.

"They're perfect," Lisa declared, and everybody agreed.

Then she deftly unfolded three wire coat hangers and quickly covered them with white felt. The blind mice now had canes to walk with. The final touch would be sunglasses, and Mrs. Lonetree said the girls were just going to have to do that themselves. Lisa, Stevie, and Carole thought that was more than fair. Then, while Mrs. Lonetree was adjusting the old gingham dress to create a farmer's-wife outfit for Kate, Christine took the "mice" into the bathroom, where they could all practice applying whiskers with an eyebrow pencil.

"Should they curl?" Stevie asked.

"I don't think so," Lisa said. By then, though, it was too late for Stevie. Her whiskers curled all the way up to her eyebrows!

"This is just a test," Stevie reminded her friends, working hard to remove the pencil marks. "I mean, we're supposed to make our mistakes now, aren't we?"

Lisa and Carole giggled and tried their own whiskers. In the end it turned out that the best ones were just a few brief straight lines radiating from above their mouths. Soon they each had proper whiskers and assured Stevie that her unsuccessful curly whiskers were hardly visible anymore.

"Nothing a shower and a scrub-brush and some bathroom cleanser can't get off," Stevie agreed cheerfully.

"Very nice," Christine said, admiring the results of the girls' efforts. "Would you like your cheese now or later?"

"That realistic?" Lisa asked.

"Absolutely, and if you think you look good, wait until you see how Kate is looking."

When they returned to Mrs. Lonetree's workroom,

they were astonished. It was their friend Kate, all
right, but she didn't look at all as she had a mere fifteen minutes ago. She was wearing a very well-padded
gingham dress with a long skirt and a full apron. She
had a white cap on her head and a very long carving
knife in one hand. Mrs. Lonetree said her outfit would
be complete with the addition of some black leather
shoes.

"I think this particular farmer's wife is going to have
to make do with black leather riding boots. Will it
work?"

"It will be the perfect touch," Mrs. Lonetree agreed.
Then she turned to Christine. "So what's it to be for
you?" she asked.

"Mine's going to take a little longer," Christine said.
"Can we work on it later?"

"Sure," her mother agreed. "That will give me some
time now to show the girls the dollhouse."

"Oh, thank you!" Stevie said. "I was afraid you
wanted to keep it a surprise. Where is it?"

"This way," Mrs. Lonetree said, standing up from
her sewing machine. She took the girls into her pottery studio. They had seen her work before. It was very
special and very beautiful. Some shelves had pots that
she was making for tourists. She followed the authen-
tic traditional shapes and designs. The ones she was
prouder of, however, were more modern interpreta-

tions of the traditional Native American pots. Carole
and Lisa looked to see the new items she was working
on. Lisa had taken pottery lessons for a while and had
an idea of how difficult the work was. She really admired Mrs. Lonetree's skill. She was about to say so
when the first gasp of delight came from Stevie, whose
eyes had gone straight to the dollhouse.

"Oh, wow!" Stevie said, hurrying to where the dollhouse stood.

Carole and Lisa joined her and agreed with her
completely.

There, in the middle of the studio, was the dollhouse. It was a perfect model of an adobe pueblo—a
Southwest Native American home. A pueblo was es-
sentially a box with steps on one side leading to the
flat roof. There was only one entrance to the pueblo
and that was from the top, via ladder. Since this was a
dollhouse, Mrs. Lonetree had designed it so the whole
thing opened in the center with a hinge to reveal the
inside.

There were simple furnishings with traditional designs and patterns. A shelf near the cooking area held
a complete array of miniature pots and bowls—just
like the ones Mrs. Lonetree made for the tourists.
There was a wall hanging, a woven rug, in traditional
patterns. A rough-hewn table held miniature weapons
used by the Native Americans of the old days—

knives, a bow, and even some very tiny arrows that actually had feathers on the shafts!

There were small wooden cooking utensils as well as gardening tools.

"It's perfect!" Stevie said.

"How can you bear to give it away?" asked Lisa.

Mrs. Lonetree smiled. "I had fun making it," she said. "Now somebody should have fun playing with it. I suppose I *could* have made some dolls, but . . ."

"Don't even think of it," Stevie said. "You've already done about a hundred times more than anybody could possibly ask. And if you want to know what I think, I think donating this incredibly beautiful work of art to benefit the after-school program at the reservation school is just about perfect."

"I kind of thought the same thing," Mrs. Lonetree said. "Those kids need every bit of help they can get. So, with your clever planning and my pots and sewing machine, we'll do well by them, won't we?"

"The best we can," Stevie said.

Lisa had a little chill right then. From the moment she'd heard about the Halloween Fair, she'd always known that it was for a good cause. Hearing how strongly Mrs. Lonetree felt made it seem even more important. It was one thing to know that you were involved in a good cause. It was another to understand, truly, that real people were going to get real benefit from it. Knowing how much work, love, and pride Mrs. Lonetree was giving to their efforts on behalf of the after-school program made Lisa see her entire trip out West in a much clearer light. She felt even better about herself and her friends.

The girls would have liked to have stayed at the Lonetrees', maybe even have a chance to play with the dollhouse a bit, but Kate reminded them that her mother was counting on their help serving dinner, and they had to get back to The Bar None.

The girls packed up their costumes, put them in their saddlebags, and got ready for the trip back home. They all thanked Mrs. Lonetree profusely for her help—in every possible way—and they remounted their horses for the final leg of their journey.

The Bar None was a short distance, perhaps two miles, across country from the Lonetrees' house. It was a trip the girls, especially Kate, had made many times, in dark and daylight. They felt safe and sure about their journey.

It had been a long and busy day, following an even longer and busier day. They rode together without talking, just enjoying the journey and thinking how welcome a good meal and a warm bunk were going to be very soon.

Lisa loved the countryside. At first look it had seemed barren to her, but now she knew better. The rocks and mountains were home for many creatures who managed to make meals of the brush and cactus that covered the land. Part of the trail back to The Bar None led through what felt like a gully between two craggy hills. One of those hills rose nearly straight up from the desert floor. A movement at the top of it caught Lisa's eye. She looked up. There, standing on a flat area at the edge of the hill, was the stallion, now clearly riderless. His herd was not in sight. He was completely silhouetted by the moonlight that streamed from behind him.

Lisa drew her horse to a halt to look, just look. Around her, her friends did the same, for they'd all seen him at the same moment.

The stallion rose then, rearing regally on his hind legs. His forelegs pawed eagerly at the vast expanse of sky in front of him. A breeze lifted his mane, brushing it back. The sight took Lisa's breath away.

The horse landed back on all fours. Without hesitation he turned around and disappeared down the other side of the hill.

"You've just *got* to have him," Stevie said.

Kate nodded, unable to speak.

CHOCOLATE HAD PICKED up a stone in her shoe on the way back from Christine's. Lisa had to get it out, or the horse's hoof would be tender and painful by morning.

Stevie, Carole, and Kate hurried to help Phyllis serve dinner while Lisa worked at Chocolate's hoof with the pick.

She'd removed plenty of stones and usually thought of it as a sort of a challenge. As long as her horse wasn't upset, Lisa was willing to work away at it. Chocolate seemed to understand completely that Lisa was doing this for her benefit. She didn't even flinch while Lisa tried to dig under the stone.

"Need help?"

Lisa looked up to find John standing there.

"No, I think I can do it," she said. "It's just that this stone is lodged in there something awful. It's Chocolate who may need help."

John stood by the mare's head and began patting her. She seemed to welcome the assurance.

"There's a sharp point on the stone, and it's stuck in a ridge or something in the shoe. The only good news here is that the part that's pushing on Chocolate's foot is round and smooth. All I need to do then is to"—she gritted her teeth, grunted, shifted the angle of the pick, and worried it back around the stone—"get this thing just so that"—she had it; she eased the handle of the pick until she felt the resistance of the stone, then with a swift and smooth motion she flexed the tool—"the stone will"—it popped out—"pop out," she said proudly.

"Nice work," John said.

Lisa lowered Chocolate's foot and patted the mare affectionately. Chocolate regarded her and then blinked. Lisa was pretty sure that was as close as she was going to get to a thank-you from Chocolate. "You're welcome," she told the horse. Then she unhooked the lead rope from Chocolate's halter and slapped her flank gently, telling the mare it was time to run free—until tomorrow. Chocolate obeyed willingly.

Lisa turned to John, then, though she didn't really know what to say to him. This boy had a way of turning up when she least expected him.

"You did a good job with the crepe paper this afternoon," she said. That sounded pretty lame to her, but it was the best she could come up with right then.

"Yeah, and you did a wonderful job holding the ladder," he returned. She shrugged and blushed. It was clear that John wasn't the kind of boy who would let her get away with being lame. She wished she hadn't made the remark about the crepe paper, but it was too late to take it back, and John was on to something else.

"I want to show you something," he said. "Come with me."

Before she could say anything, he took her hand and led her into the barn. Lisa wasn't used to having a boy hold her hand. It gave her a nice chill and made her knees feel a little funny—a little off balance. John did seem to have a way of making her feel off balance no matter what he did.

"What is it?" she asked.

"Remember the mare?"

"Of course."

"The vet was wrong."

"About what?"

"About how long it would be until she foaled." John drew to a stop at the box stall where he had been sitting with the edgy mare just a little less than twenty-four hours earlier. The stall was still occupied, but now there was more than just a mare. There was a mare and a foal.

"Oh, when was it born?" she asked breathlessly.

"This afternoon. Isn't she a cute filly?"

Lisa nodded. The filly seemed to know that they were talking about her. She looked curiously at Lisa, her bright eyes taking in everything. Then she flicked her skinny little gray tail and turned all her attention to her mother. It was, after all, supper time.

"She's adorable!" Lisa said. "Thanks for showing her to me."

"I knew you'd love her."

Lisa crossed her forearms on the top of the door to the stall and put her chin on her wrist so she could watch the filly and the mare.

"You know, a newborn horse is an amazing creature," she observed. "They usually stand up within a few minutes of being born and walk almost immediately. When I compare that to how long it takes the average human to do those things, it's not hard to understand why horses are so much more fun to ride."

John laughed. "I never thought of it that way, but you're probably right."

"Were you here when she was born?" Lisa asked.

"I was," he said. "I'm glad I was, too. The mare didn't turn out to need any help, but I wanted to be here in case she did. The vet said she had more than a week to go, but I didn't think he was right."

"How did you learn so much about horses and foaling?" Lisa asked.

John seemed to hesitate, but he answered. "My mother was a horse breeder," he told her. "She taught me everything I know. It's part of the legacy she left me."

"Left you?" Lisa asked.

"She's dead," he said. And the way he said it warned Lisa she shouldn't ask any more. His tone of voice was like a door slamming in her face. This was the mystery, she recalled. It had something to do with John's mother. There probably was an answer, but Lisa wasn't going to get it from John. She was slightly annoyed that he trusted her so little. She wanted to change the subject, and she wanted to take the upper hand.

"We saw the stallion again tonight. Twice in fact."

"Still running free?"

"As you very well know," she said.

"Why should I know?" he asked. "I don't know when they round up the horses for the adoption."

"Very good," Lisa said. "Nice try. But we saw you. You were there when the coyotes were calling."

John looked puzzled. "When was that?" he asked.

"About four-thirty," Lisa said. "Just about exactly the same time you climbed on the stallion's back and rode him."

"Somebody was riding him?"

"Yes, John. We saw somebody—or some*thing*—mounted on the stallion."

John was silent for a moment. Then he spoke. "I've heard talk of incidents like that," he said.

"Come on, John," Lisa said. She was getting a little tired of his mysterious tale and wished he would just loosen up and tell her the truth. "We saw you."

"You saw somebody," he said. "I believe you. But you didn't see me. I was here. I came home on the school bus, and I never left the mare's side. The filly was born at five o'clock this afternoon."

Lisa looked at the filly, and she knew that John would never have abandoned that mare in the middle of foaling just to play a trick on some girls. No way.

# 8

EVEN LATER, AFTER it was all over, Stevie and her friends couldn't believe how much work they got done by the time the fair opened. It seemed like a mad rush to finish everything, and Stevie wondered if they'd ever manage to get their own costumes on, but somehow they did it. At exactly eighteen seconds before noon on Saturday, they were ready. They were still breathless from the dash, but three blind mice and the farmer's wife all stood in line waiting for the first guests to arrive at the high school basement.

"Where's Christine?" Lisa asked.

"She's still getting dressed," Kate said. "She was very mysterious about her costume. All I know is that her mother seemed pleased with all the work she'd done."

"Greetings, girls." It was a boy's voice, but it was a man's costume. Stevie looked, gasped, and giggled. It had to be John, but there was no true way to recognize him. He was dressed as the headless horseman! He was wearing black jeans, black boots, and a very large black turtleneck that rose up over his head. Stevie suspected he was using one or two sets of football shoulder pads to hold it up, and the effect was really good. He'd also managed to find a black cloak with a bright red lining, which helped mask the slight oddity of his big, high shoulders and his relatively small, short arms.

"Has anybody seen my friend Ichabod?" he asked.

Lisa laughed. "I think he'll be here in a few minutes. Why don't you join us on the receiving line and scare the daylights out of all the kids who are about to arrive."

"Gladly," he said, standing next to her.

"You all have done a *wonderful* job," Phyllis Devine said in the moment of quiet before the storm when the doors would open. "I think we'll have a great financial success, but I know that, no matter what, we're going to be running a party here this afternoon that no child is going to forget. It wouldn't be the same without all the help you have given. So I want to thank you all— say, where's Christine?"

"I'm right here," she said, entering the room from behind them. When the girls turned to look, they were stunned. Christine Lonetree was dressed as the young Indian boy from the story that John had told. She was wearing a completely white outfit that was topped by a white cape. On the back of the cape Mrs. Lonetree had painted a flying eagle.

Lisa's eyes flitted to John, still standing next to her. She wondered what he thought. She couldn't see his face behind the long neck of his "headless" top, but she could hear his low whistle of admiration.

Before anybody could say anything, the doors flew open and young children filled the room. The rush was on!

CAROLE LOVED BEING in charge of pony rides. She was always happiest around any kind of a horse, but now it was even truer because the kids were having such fun. Most of these children were familiar with horses, so that made the job a lot easier. Even better, though, was the fact that they were all in costume and were having their pictures taken by Frank Devine. The pony was sporting a witch's pointed hat, and it seemed to go perfectly with the costume that each child wore—everything from the Incredible Hulk to Sleeping Beauty (snoring loudly). Carole saw to it that each child had a fun ride, got a good picture, and learned a new fact about horses.

"You tell their age by how their teeth have worn," she said to one rider.

"There's no such thing as a white horse, just gray, no matter how white the horse looks," another learned.

"English riders have their stirrups shorter than Western," one child heard.

"Horses don't have any nerves in their manes, so you can hold it for balance if you need to, and it won't hurt the horse. Of course, that's not good riding style, but it may be excellent safety sometime!"

All of the kids seemed to like what they were learning as well as what they were doing. Although Carole knew she wanted to work with horses for the rest of her life, she'd always thought her choices were among owner, breeder, trainer, and vet. Today she was having so much fun teaching, she was beginning to think she ought to add instructor to the list.

"Smile now," she told the Teenage Mutant Ninja Turtle in the saddle. Somewhere under the costume she was sure the child was smiling a lot.

"WHAT HAPPENED TO YOU?" Kate asked Christine.

"I think I just got trampled by two sugarplum fairies and a robot," Christine explained, rubbing her shoulder, which had gotten slightly bruised. "Those fairies were determined to get to the costume parade!"

Kate giggled.

When Christine's shoulder stopped throbbing, she laughed, too. "It means they're having a good time, and that's what this is about," she said philosophically. "At least I think that's what that means." She rubbed her shoulder again.

"What those two fairies don't know, however, is that you're one of the judges of the costume parade!"

"I am?"

"You are now," Kate said, tugging at Christine's cape. "And there's work to be done."

"OF COURSE IT'S your pumpkin, and you can do whatever you want," Phyllis Devine said to a teary-eyed ghost. "It doesn't matter what that vampire next to you says. If you want a happy pumpkin, you get a happy pumpkin."

"Really?"

"Really."

The ghost turned to the vampire and stuck her tongue out at him.

"JUST GUESS," STEVIE said. "You really can't possibly count all the candy corns just by looking at the jar. You're supposed to *guess*."

"Is it more than two thousand?" the panda in front of her asked.

"Guess," Stevie repeated. "Actually, you can guess as many times as you want. It only costs you a quarter for each guess, and the more guesses you make, the better chance you have of winning the dollhouse."

Once again Stevie pointed to the photograph of the adobe dollhouse that had been getting so much attention. The panda reached into her pocket and pulled out six tickets worth twenty-five cents each. Then she took six slips of paper, carefully wrote her name on the top of each, and wrote 2,000; 2,001; 2,002; 2,003; 2,004; and 2,005.

"I'm pretty sure it's more than two thousand," she told Stevie earnestly as she tucked her entry forms into the cigar box.

"I hope you win," Stevie said. She meant it, too.

MRS. LONETREE HANDED a clean paintbrush to Superman.

"You can paint whatever you'd like on our mural, but a lot of the children have chosen to paint themselves, in their costumes. I think a nice place for Superman would be—"

"Right here," he said, pointing to the top of the mural. "I can fly, you know."

"I know," said Mrs. Lonetree. "Let me get you a

chair to stand on so you can put yourself in just the right place!" She did that. She also brought him the red, blue, and yellow paints so he'd make himself the right colors. The mural, a piece of brown wrapping paper that was eight feet tall and twenty-five feet long, was taped to one very long wall of the basement. Anybody who wanted to was invited to come and paint anything they wanted on it. It was another one of Stevie's bright ideas, and it was working beautifully. The youngest kids weren't very good at drawing ghosts and goblins, but to most viewers' eyes, the scribbles of color were just as pretty as the neat ballerina next to them.

"Can I have some orange?" Superman asked.

"Sure," Mrs. Lonetree said. "What's going to be orange?"

"Oh, it's the sun that Superman is melting in order to be able to fry some bad guys who are trying to steal all the television sets in Metropolis so nobody can watch cartoons. . . ."

He was interrupted by a little girl. "Hey! Don't get your old sun all over my balloon that's supposed to be taking Dorothy back to Kansas!"

Superman promised to be careful.

Mrs. Lonetree smiled. This mural will be very special, she thought to herself as she went to fetch the orange paint.

• • •

*AAAAAAAARRRHHHHHH!*

It was a bloodcurdling scream—just exactly the kind everybody wanted to hear coming out of the horror house. It was immediately followed by joyful giggles.

"Don't do that again!" one child chided.

"What? I didn't do anything!"

"You didn't?"

That was the sort of conversation Lisa had been hearing ever since she'd taken her position behind the black curtain in the horror house. Her job was to reach out and tickle kids from behind after they'd passed her. They somehow always thought it had been done by whomever they were with.

"No," the companion said.

"You did *too!*"

Then she'd scoot up a bit, reach out, and tickle the other person.

"What was that?"

"It wasn't me!"

That was when Lisa would scream. It was more fun than she could remember having for a long time, and the best part of it was that the kids loved it, too. Usually by that time they'd figured out that they weren't alone, and they'd start laughing. Some of them could hardly walk because they were laughing so hard. Their enjoyment was a real tribute to Stevie. If Lisa had ever doubted it, she knew for sure now the truth of the notion that Stevie was a genius. Nobody else could have possibly come up with such a wonderfully scary and funny horror house as this. And that was before the kids even got to the part where the vacuum cleaners blew out at them, or where they landed on Styrofoam peanuts.

"Now follow me *this* way," came a familiar voice. It was John. He had volunteered to be a guide in the horror house. Each pair of children going through the house had a guide just to be sure they didn't get lost or too scared. Also, it was a way to guarantee that they wouldn't *counter*attack!

Lisa reached out at just the right minute and tickled one child. Then, as the argument got going between the visitors, she tickled the other. Pretty soon they were both laughing. The headless horseman seemed to turn in her direction, and if she hadn't been sure that she could not have possibly seen it, she would have sworn that the headless horseman had winked at her.

Once again she was struck by what an interesting mix of characteristics John Brightstar was. He had seemed so serious and distant last night, and now he was acting as if he didn't have a care in the world. She was so intrigued by her observations that she almost forgot to tickle a leprechaun.

•  •  •

IT FILLED STEVIE'S heart with joy to look at the over-stuffed cigar box of entries for the Kount the Kandy Korn Kontest. Mrs. Lonetree's dollhouse had brought every single child to the table. Several of the children had spent as long looking at the photograph as they had looking at the jar. Stevie particularly recalled two girls who had invented an imaginary family and had begun playing with them in the dollhouse just as they stood at the table. Whoever won it was going to be the happiest child in Two Mile Creek. Now all Stevie had to do was be sure that everybody who wanted to enter the contest had a chance and then figure out who had won.

No, she realized with a start. That *wasn't* all she had to do. She had to get the dollhouse as well. She felt the blood drain from her face. How could she have forgotten? Mrs. Lonetree had had to walk over this morning. Christine had ridden her horse. Neither could bring the dollhouse. Stevie had promised to call Frank and ask him to stop by the Lonetrees' and bring it on his way, but she'd completely forgotten. Now she was about to have a winner, and she didn't have a prize.

She'd spent too much time watching how excited the children were at the prospect of winning. After seeing those faces she couldn't tell the winner he or she was going to have to wait. Somehow she had to get the dollhouse back to the fair before the winner was announced—in exactly one hour.

Stevie looked around for help. Everybody was busy. Carole was still taking kids on rides. Mrs. Lonetree was up to her elbows in clay, showing a group of fascinated children how to make miniature bowls. Phyllis Devine was overseeing the cupcake decorating. Kate was turning masked kids in circles so they could pin the stem on the pumpkin, and Christine was doing something with two sugarplum fairies. Nobody could help Stevie. She was going to have to do this herself. But what was she going to do?

Stevie realized that Mr. Lonetree wasn't there. That probably meant he was at the ranch and would be able to drive the dollhouse over to the school. It wasn't a long distance. All she had to do was call.

She dug into her pocket, found change, and located the students' pay phone on the first floor of the school.

*I'm sorry. We are experiencing technical difficulties. Please try to place your call again later.*

She checked the number. She had it right. She tried again.

*I'm sorry. . . .*

For how long could there be technical difficulties?

*I'm sor—*

She couldn't wait. She didn't have time to wait. She

had to do something. The only thing she could think of was to go to the Lonetrees' house herself and hope that Mr. Lonetree would be there to bring her and the dollhouse back.

She tucked the quarter back into her pocket. She would ride Stewball there. She knew the way. It wouldn't take long. But she had to tell somebody what she was doing.

She found Christine standing outside the girls' bathroom.

"The sugarplum fairies had to go," she explained. "I'm waiting for them, and then I promised to take them through the horror house."

Stevie wasn't sure she understood exactly how Christine had gotten to be the girls' personal attendant at the fair, but Christine said it had something to do with a consolation prize for the costume parade. That made some sense—not much, but enough.

Stevie explained her dilemma. "Do you think your dad's at home?" she asked.

"I'm sure he will be," she said. "I'm also sure he'll drive you back. Too bad about the phones, but it happens. Do you know the trail?"

"Yes," Stevie assured her. "It's not hard to follow. I'm sure I'll be fine."

"I'm sure you will be, too. But it's going to be cold. Do you have a jacket?"

94

"No, just this sweatshirt," Stevie said.

"Well, it's not much, but here, take my cloak. It should help some with the breezes."

"Thanks," Stevie said, slipping the cloak over her shoulders. Then, when the girls'-room door opened, Stevie got a look at herself in the mirror. There she was, one blind field mouse, wearing a silvery white cloak. It seemed about right for a Halloween ride.

9

STEWBALL SHOOK HIS head and snorted. Stevie thought that was his way of saying he was happy to be out of the corral and out on a trail. Stevie agreed. It was quite dark outside, and it was cool, but it was pleasant. She leaned forward and patted the horse on his neck just to show that she felt the same way. Then she nudged him a little, and they began trotting. Much as she was enjoying the ride, she didn't want to be gone too long from the fair. Besides, she couldn't wait to find out who won the adobe dollhouse.

There was a screeching sound. Stewball's ears flicked eagerly. Stevie looked to where she'd heard the noise, but saw nothing.

"It must have been some kind of bird or something,

boy," she told the horse. "I mean, just because it's Halloween . . ." Her voice trailed off.

It *was* Halloween. That was supposed to be a night when ghosts and ghouls roamed free. Witches flew through the sky, casting spells. Vampires ruled the blood supply. Headless horsemen thundered along roadways after unwary victims. It was a night of unfettered evil. . . .

"Oh, stop it," Stevie told herself. She spoke out loud as if trying to be sure she heeded her own words. "It's just another date on the calendar. There's nothing special about it. It's just the end of October and . . . and, uh . . ."

She saw something. She'd definitely seen something. Stewball felt her tense up and took it as a signal. He stopped. That wasn't what she wanted at all. She wanted to get out of there! She clicked her tongue and tapped him with her heels. He began walking again, very slowly. Stevie got a grip on herself and looked around cautiously.

She had left the road and was now crossing the open land. It was the same trail she'd followed with her friends just over twenty-four hours ago. But it didn't look the same at all. Now that she was alone, it didn't look beautiful and exciting. It looked barren and dangerous. Stevie shivered.

There was the screech again. She looked up to

where the sound had come from this time. A dark shadow passed across the full moon, which stood just above the horizon. Stevie sighed with relief. It was a bird, probably some kind of owl, since they were night hunters. It had a big wingspan to be sure, but it wasn't big enough to be a threat to Stevie or Stewball.

"Come on, boy. Let's just get this over with, okay?" They rode on.

There were the familiar landmarks. She spotted the promontory where they'd seen the stallion rear. It was still outlined by the bright moon. This time there was no sign of the stallion, and what had appeared as an interesting piece of landscape when she'd been with her friends now seemed to be merely stark. Her mind was flooded with an image of riding the stallion to the edge of the cliff. He reared, she held on tightly. His weight shifted. She grabbed his mane. His feet slipped. . . .

"Oh, stop it!" she said again.

Something grabbed her hair. She screamed, and Stewball started. Stevie managed to hold the reins, and the horse stopped. She flailed wildly to free her hair from the unearthly creature that held it, harder and tighter with every motion. The more she struggled, the harder it was—until Stewball took two steps backward. That was when the tension was released on the branch and Stevie's hair was freed. Still shaking, she looked over her shoulder to be sure. That's all it was—just a branch.

"I think we'd better get going," she said to Stewball. Without further ado, he picked up a trot. Stevie was beginning to get the feeling that this exciting solo night ride couldn't be over fast enough.

She needed something to give her courage and decided that the best something would be a distraction. She decided to try singing. Horses liked singing. Stewball would probably get courage from it, too. Also, Stewball wasn't likely to be much of a music critic, so he wouldn't care if she hit a wrong note. She knew just the song to sing for him.

> *"Old Stewball was a racehorse,*
> *And I wish he were mine.*
> *He never drank water;*
> *He always drank wi-ine!"*

She smiled at her choice. Not only was it good to sing a song about her very own horse, it was also a song with dozens of verses and would keep her mind and her voice occupied for miles.

> *"His bridle was silver,*
> *His mane it was gold.*

99

> *And the worth of his saddle*
> *Has never been to-old!*

> *To-old!"*

Who was that? Stevie's heart jumped.
"Hello!"
*Hello!*
Her voice bounced back at her off the mountain-side.

"Oh, swell," Stevie said, disgusted with herself. "I've gotten so spooked that I'm fighting off branches and getting scared of a dumb old echo. Come on, Stewball. Let's get back to work." She took a deep breath and began singing again.

> *"I bet on the gray mare,*
> *I bet on the bay.*
> *If I'd've bet on old Stewball,*
> *I'd be a free man today!"*

It wasn't working. The singing didn't make her feel any better, and she knew that Stewball could feel her tension right through the saddle. If Stevie had learned one thing about horses, it was that you couldn't fool them. They knew when their riders knew what they were doing. If they sensed uncertainty, they were likely to decide to take charge. Stewball began to prance restlessly. Stevie had to do something about that. She brought him up to a trot, and then, when they were on open and smooth land, she decided to let him lope. That would have the advantage of covering the distance faster and would let Stewball work out some knots.

At first Stewball seemed as glad as Stevie was to be going faster. Then something happened. A coyote howled. Two more joined it, and one of those was very close. No matter how well trained a horse was, he was still a creature of the wild, and in the wild a threatened horse had two choices: He could fight or he could flee. Most would flee. At night, unprotected by the presence of a herd, Stewball's innate senses took over his domesticated side. He felt the immediate threat of the presence of a predator. His instinct left him no choice. He took off.

Stevie was totally unprepared for it. Suddenly the horse who had been loping along pleasantly was racing. The three-beat gait turned to a four-beat gait, and at that it was so fast it was almost indistinguishable from a one-beat gait. Stewball was really covering ground.

He veered off the trail, frantically seeking safety. He leapt over a small cactus, turned sharply around a rock, and fled. Through all this Stevie held on, trying desperately to regain control of her horse. She lost a foothold in one of her stirrups and couldn't tighten up on the reins. With every step she came closer and closer to falling off. When Stewball took another turn to the right and shifted immediately to the left, further spooked by some unseen danger, that was it for Stevie. She flew up and out of the saddle and landed smack on her bottom. It hurt like crazy, but she was too angry to cry. All she could do was watch the retreating rear of her very frightened horse.

When the dust settled, she stood up, wiped her seat tentatively, decided it was going to be a good thing she wouldn't have to look at the bruise she was sure to have, and began walking. She didn't sing this time. She just grumbled.

"Here I am, in the middle of nowhere, walking when I should be riding, heading for Christine's house, so I can see if I can find somebody who will drive me back to the fair. All because I forgot to call earlier and because the phones weren't working right and there is a little child back at the high school who is going to be the happiest kid in town if and when I get back with the dollhouse, but I don't know if I can, except that just knowing some child is going to own that makes me want to keep on walking in spite of the fact that my stupid horse . . ."

She went on like that. It kept her focused on what

she was really doing, but it didn't change the fact that she wasn't exactly thrilled with the circumstances. It also kept her mind off the spooky things that had bothered her before—the owl and the branch and her own Halloween-y thoughts.

". . . and I don't know what I'll do if Mr. Lonetree isn't there, but somehow I'll find a way because, after all, my friends and I have traveled a couple thousand miles to be able to do this, so how could I possibly give up when I'm within about a half . . ."

A noise.

"Oh, come on, Stevie. The night is full of noises. Is this another echo scaring you?"

There it was again. She stopped.

It wasn't an echo, but when she listened to it, she wished it were. She wished it were an owl screeching or a witch or a vampire or any of a dozen imaginary things that had frightened her before, because this wasn't imaginary. This was real. This was dangerous. It was a rattlesnake.

Stevie had heard them before. She'd even seen them. She'd seen one kill. She froze, aware that the slightest movement could attract the snake's attention. She waited.

The sound came again. But where was it coming from?

There were several rocky places right around her as

well as a bush, any one of which could be hiding the viper.

Again, she heard it. Was it to the right? Or was it from straight ahead? Or was it that it came from the left, but the sound bounced off the rocks to the right? Nearby? Far? Would it strike? Would it hurt? Would it kill?

Terror took over. Stevie had never felt anything like it. She had nowhere to turn and no hope for escape. The terror filled her heart and her lungs. She gasped for breath, and when she got it, she screamed, long, loud, and hard. When she was done, she screamed some more, hearing only the echo of her own voice—and the rattle, constant, now drumming in her ears. Where? When?

Then there was another sound. It was the sound of hoofbeats. Stewball?

Stevie's eyes flicked upward. It wasn't Stewball. It was the stallion with the nick in his ear. There was a rider on his back, cloaked in white. A long and strong arm reached out to her. She reached up. In a smooth motion she was drawn up behind the rider and they flew across the desert, away from the snake, away from all danger.

Stevie clung to the rider with all her strength, not speaking a word. She couldn't have, anyway. She couldn't even utter a thank-you. She was shaking too hard. She could still hear the rattles. She could still hear the tones of her own screams echoing off the hills.

The stallion drew to a halt in front of the Lonetrees' house. Stevie dismounted, took a deep breath, and tried to think how she could thank John for being there just when she needed him the most. But the horse and rider turned and rode off, as quickly as they had come, without saying a word. Stevie shook her head and promised herself she would thank him the next time she saw him. For now, though, all she could do was look at that shiny white cloak he wore with the beautifully embroidered eagle on the back. John really did love practical jokes—he must have borrowed the cape Mrs. Lonetree had made for Christine so his outfit would be perfect for the part.

A night breeze cut across the land then. Stevie shivered and wrapped her arms around herself. That was when she remembered that *she* was wearing Christine's white cloak—and the eagle on Christine's cloak was painted, not embroidered with feathers. If the rider was John, this wasn't just a hoax, it was a very elaborate hoax. And if it wasn't John, just who—or what— was it?

"STEVIE? IS THAT YOU?"

The words gave Stevie a start. Then she realized it was Mr. Lonetree.

"Yes," she said, still confused by what had happened.

"I was looking for you. Your horse showed up here a few minutes ago, and then Christine called. She said something about the phones being broken for a while. Anyway, I'm glad you're safe. What happened?"

Now *there* was a question.

It took Stevie a while to pull all of the pieces together and to tell the story of her ride across the country-side without making herself sound like a fool or a fraidy cat. When Mr. Lonetree asked her how she'd gotten away from the rattlesnake, and assured her that she wasn't a fool or a fraidy cat to have been frightened by that snake, she found herself telling him about the silvery stallion Kate wanted to adopt and its connection to the story John had told the girls in the bunkhouse that night.

"Yes, the tale of White Eagle," Mr. Lonetree said. "I know it well. It's a story our people have told for generations. Nobody quite believes it's true, but everybody loves the tale."

"It's so romantic!" Stevie said. "I guess John was just trying to tell us a romantic eerie story for Halloween."

Mr. Lonetree looked confused. "Never would have thought of that story as eerie," he said.

"You might if you were thinking of owning the horse," Stevie told him. "We thought he made it up just to keep Kate from owning the stallion."

"Oh," said Mr. Lonetree. "I wouldn't have thought of it that way. See, to our people the traditional idea of ownership is very different from the way the Europeans who settled the land of America saw it. To us, all animals and land are something we have the honor to use for a while, but never own. Oh, sure, in America of the twentieth century, I have a deed for my property and a title to my car, but it's contrary to our tradition. I'm sure John Brightstar feels the same way. Even if one does 'own' a wild animal, it's not ownership in the sense you mean. I doubt he was trying to keep Kate from owning the stallion. I suspect he was rather saying that no matter what, she couldn't. Besides, Stevie, you and I are forgetting for a moment that it's just a story."

"Maybe," Stevie agreed reluctantly.

"Hey, we've got to get you back to the high school along with the dollhouse. Let's put your horse in the back of the van so you'll have transportation home—by the roadway, if you please."

"I promise," she said without hesitation.

THE MINUTE STEVIE walked into the party with the dollhouse, there was a hush. And then there was a rush. Everybody in the place wanted to make more guesses about the number of candies in the jar. She had a line of children following her before she could even get to the table. She wanted to tell her friends about what had happened out on the desert, but it would have to wait. Right now they couldn't take the twenty-five-cent tickets and hand out the guess slips fast enough. It was wonderful!

They even ended up agreeing to let the children put in guesses half an hour longer than they'd originally intended, just to make sure everybody who wanted to could enter the contest. Finally, when the last child had filled out the last slip, she took the jar of candies and the box of guesses out of the main room and went in search of a quiet place where she could sort all the entries and find the one or more that had the right number. The correct answer was known only to Phyllis Devine, who had written it on a piece of paper, put it in an envelope, and placed it at the bottom of the jar. Stevie thought that maybe she'd have to eat a lot of the candies in order to get to it, too.

The most quiet and private spot around was the horror house, which had been shut down. She entered, turned on some lights, and pulled up a chair to the table where the peeled grapes and cold pasta had been so terrifying to little visitors so recently. They didn't look particularly frightening in the light. Nor did they look appetizing. Stevie emptied the bowls in a nearby garbage can and went to work.

**11**

"HOLD THE LADDER steady now," John said from above.

"Don't worry," Lisa assured him. "I got plenty of practice at it when you were putting the crepe paper *up*. I don't think I've lost all my skills now that you're taking it down."

"Thanks," he said, dropping a large handful of crepe paper on the floor. Lisa scooped it up and put it in the garbage, all without letting go of the ladder.

Although other parts of the fair were continuing, the horror house was closed for the season, and the two of them had appointed themselves the committee to take it apart. It was a lot easier than putting it all together, and it seemed like a nice way to finish the day. At last it was relatively quiet, and there, in the small rooms they'd made for the horror house, it was even a little cozy—if you didn't mind crepe paper drifting down from above every once in a while.

"There, that's the last of that bunch," John said, climbing down. "I think there's some more in the next section, though."

"Not much," Lisa said. "Most of it got pulled down by the kids who were running to get away from me."

"You were great," he said. "I mean, all the kids I brought through were more scared when you were tickling them than at any other point—even more than when they slid into the Styrofoam."

"You weren't bad yourself—as a headless horseman, I mean. You scared a lot of the kids with that costume."

"Maybe, but I'm glad to be rid of those shoulder pads. I always wondered if I should be going out for football. Now I know for sure I couldn't possibly stand all that weight."

"Correct me if I'm wrong, but it seems to me that most football players only wear one set of shoulder pads at a time, right? And I also think they make their jerseys so that their heads stick out the top?"

John smiled at her joke. "I guess so, but I still think I'll stick to lacrosse. It's more my style, and you aren't as likely to get totally beaten up. Anyway, I didn't like scaring the kids too much. I know Halloween is supposed to be a little scary, but some of them were very frightened by me. I was glad to take the costume off for them, too."

"You're good with the kids," Lisa said. "Have you had experience? I mean, have you got younger brothers and sisters?"

Lisa was sorry the instant she'd asked the question. Of course he didn't have any younger brothers and sisters or they'd be at The Bar None with John and his dad. John seemed to be sensitive to any questions about his family. She wished she'd thought before she spoke.

"I did," he answered, surprising her.

"You did?" she couldn't help asking.

"I—" he sat down on the bottom step of the ladder. "I did, once," he said, completing his sentence.

Lisa wasn't sure if he regretted giving the information or if he really wanted to talk.

"You don't have to . . . ," she began.

"But I want to," he blurted suddenly. "Somehow I think you'll understand."

Would she? She didn't know. So far, she felt only confusion. She waited.

"I did have a sister. Her name was Gaylin. She was a wonderful child, always happy, always laughing. Then one day Gaylin was sick. She was very sick and there was no doctor nearby. My father had to drive my mother and Gaylin to the hospital. I came along, too. I sat in the front seat with Dad. Mother was in the back. Gaylin lay on the backseat next to her with her head on Mother's lap. She was so sick she was sweating with her fever. Dad knew it was bad, and he knew Gaylin's life depended on his ability to drive. He drove fast, as fast as he could, and still it didn't seem like it was fast enough. But it turned out to be too fast, because when a deer ran across the road, Dad tried to stop and swerved to avoid it. He missed the deer but ran the car right off the edge of the road and down a shallow ravine. He and I were okay. We'd had our seatbelts on. But Mother and Gaylin weren't so lucky."

Lisa gulped, understanding his pain.

"There was a police inquiry," John continued. "Some people said Dad had been drinking, but it wasn't true. There was a question, though, and there was talk. Plenty of it. Anybody could feel sorry for a man whose wife and daughter were killed in a car accident. Nobody would pity a man who'd killed them. It wasn't Dad's fault. Even the police concluded that. That didn't stop the rumors, though."

"Oh, John," Lisa began. "It must have been awful. . . ." It seemed like such a weak thing to say, but she meant it.

"It was," he said. "It still is, too, especially for Dad.

He doesn't drink, never did, but sometimes it seems like he might as well. He just withdraws, sleeps all the time. That's where he was the other night when you found me with the mare. He should have been there, but he wasn't. So I was just filling in."

Lisa reached for John's hand. She wanted to give him comfort, but she also wanted to be close to him. His hand was big and strong and warm. She squeezed it affectionately.

"You must miss them both," she said.

"I do. But in some ways I still have them, here in my heart, I mean. Every time I see a happy child, I feel I am with Gaylin again. And my mother? Well, I remember her through the stories she used to tell us. She was the great-granddaughter of a chief, and it was her family's responsibility to keep the hearth and carry the traditions to each succeeding generation."

"You mean like the story about the young lovers and the stallion? She told you that?"

"It was her favorite. She swore it was true, too. She lived all of her life believing that story—believing that no matter what else happened, there was always the stallion to help those who tried to do good things for our people. Sometimes I'm sure it was White Eagle who carried her and Gaylin out of the car . . ."

"How beautiful," Lisa said.

She became aware then that John was looking at her deeply. He glanced at their hands, now clasped warmly. He stood up and reached for her other hand. Lisa gave it to him.

"Lisa, I—"

"Shhh. You don't have to say anything."

He moved closer to her. She looked up at him, wondering, hoping, knowing . . .

"Got one!" Stevie shrieked from the other side of a temporary wall.

Lisa and John looked at one another in total surprise. They had had no idea she was there!

"Got what?" Lisa asked. She was trying very hard not to sound annoyed, but it wasn't easy. If she'd had her choice of when to be interrupted by her dear friend Stevie, it would have been almost any time but then!

"Oh, is that you, Lisa? Are you there? Are you alone?" Stevie asked.

Lisa and John shared a little giggle. "I'm here with John," Lisa said, brushing the layers of curtains aside and joining Stevie in what they'd come to think of as the grape-and-spaghetti room. John followed her.

"I got a winner," Stevie told them proudly. "Look, here it is. One child got the *exact* number of candy corns that Phyllis wrote on her piece of paper. Now all I have to do is search and see if anybody else has it. I was afraid I was going to have to sort through a thousand entries to find the one that's the closest. Give me a hand, will you? You, too, John?"

"You and Lisa can do that," John said. "I think I'll finish removing the black crepe paper and see what else needs to be tidied. See you later, okay?"

"Sure," Stevie said. Then she thought for a second. This seemed like the perfect opportunity to test and see if the mysterious rider had been John. If he admitted it, that would confirm it. If he denied it, well, it almost certainly still was John. After all, who else could it be? A ghost? No way! "Thanks for helping me earlier," she said finally.

Lisa didn't know what Stevie was talking about, but there was a mischievous twinkle in Stevie's eye, and Lisa found herself a little bit jealous.

"How's that?" John asked. Apparently he didn't know what she was talking about, either. That made Lisa feel somewhat better.

"Out there?" Stevie said.

"Where?"

"In the desert? When you saved my life?"

"I don't know what you're talking about," John said.

"You don't have to keep it up anymore," Stevie said. "I mean, after all, you did deliver me safely to the Lonetrees' house."

"I did?"

"Nice try, but thanks anyway. No matter what you say, I still say thank you. You didn't give me a chance before, so now I'm saying it and I mean it."

John shrugged. "I guess you're welcome then," he said. "But I don't know why."

He slipped away. Lisa could hear him moving the ladder. She wanted to go hold it for him. She wanted to be with him, to bring back that moment of quiet and intimacy that was unlike any moment she'd ever known before in her life.

"Here, you go through this stack," Stevie said, handing her a huge pile of entry slips.

"What was that all about?" Lisa asked when she was sure John was out of their hearing.

"It was just another one of John's practical jokes," Stevie said. "Except this one was no joke and it was very practical. I'll tell you later, okay? Right now, we have to concentrate on these entry slips. Besides, I want to tell the whole story to everyone at once." Stevie looked at the entry slip on the top of her stack and scowled. "Is that 7,561 or 7,567?" she asked.

"Doesn't matter. It's not the right answer," Lisa said quickly. She wanted to pump Stevie for more information on her mysterious conversation with John, but she knew there was no point. If Stevie had decided to keep a secret—for now, anyway—wild horses, even silvery stallions, couldn't drag it out of her.

Lisa concentrated on the stack of slips in front of her.

STEVIE FELT WONDERFUL. The gigantic pile of entry slips in front of her meant she and Lisa were going to have to do a lot of work looking through them, but it also meant they made a ton of money. Mrs. Lonetree's dollhouse was perfect!

A few other things had her feeling good as well. For one thing, she had a wonderful adventure to share with her friends! For another, she was alive. She still hadn't recovered from her fright out on the trail with the rattlesnake, but she *was* alive, and she was safe. Moreover, she'd had a chance to thank John—even though he denied it, of course.

"John is one funny guy," Stevie said to Lisa.

"Yes," Lisa agreed. Stevie could have sworn her

friend sighed as she said it. She couldn't imagine why.

"How did it go in the horror house?" Stevie asked.

"What?" Lisa asked. She seemed embarrassed. Again, Stevie couldn't figure out Lisa's reaction.

"Horror house," Stevie repeated. "I heard kids screaming all afternoon. I assume that means they were having fun."

"Oh, yes, of course," Lisa said. "The kids had a fabulous time. Everything you planned worked beautifully. You are a genius, you know. About most things."

"Yes, I know," Stevie said modestly, though it crossed her mind briefly to wonder what things Lisa thought she *wasn't* a genius about. It wasn't too hard to figure out. Lisa was a straight-A student. Stevie wasn't. Stevie decided that was what Lisa meant.

They worked together in silence, now quickly sifting through the entries. They had to pause a few times because they had trouble with handwriting or wanted to share a particularly interesting entry.

"Get this," Stevie said, reading from a small slip of paper. "It says 'Even if this isn't right, please, please, please choose me because I really love the dollhouse.'"

"Is it the right number?" Lisa asked.

"Nope, and too bad," Stevie said. "I remember the child who filled it out. She's dressed as Darth Vader. She scared me, I'll tell you!"

Eventually they finished examining the last of the entries and were more than a little relieved to find that there was only one correct answer. They had no idea what they would have done if there had been more than one winner. Stevie had suggested the possibility that she might eat a candy or two until they got to another number that there was only one entry for. Fortunately, she didn't have to.

The minute Stevie and Lisa entered the main room of the basement, there was a hush. Every child there knew Stevie was in charge and what she had just been up to.

"We have a winner!" Stevie declared.

The kids gathered around.

"We certainly do," said Phyllis Devine, momentarily taking the floor from Stevie. "And the winner is the after-school program. While Stevie has been counting candies, I've been counting cash. Today's fair has earned over two thousand dollars!" Stevie could hardly believe it. She'd thought they would be lucky to make five hundred dollars.

"Now, Stevie, tell us who the winner is."

Stevie took the winning slip from Lisa. "The actual number of candies in the jar was two thousand five!" There was a gasp. Stevie had completely forgotten, but she knew who the winner was. She'd watched the little panda fill out all six slips. Two thousand five was her very last twenty-five cents!

"It's *me!*" declared the panda, dashing forward. "I won! I won!"

Stevie couldn't help grinning. Neither could anybody else who witnessed the joy.

"You absolutely did!" Stevie said, giving the little girl a hug and leading her to where her dollhouse was stored. The two of them were followed by a lot of curious and excited kids. By the time Stevie actually turned over the dollhouse to the panda, the girl was too busy making playdates with friends who wanted a chance at her newest toy to pay any attention to Stevie. It was all Stevie could do to get out of the mob. Their happiness made her feel very good. This was definitely for a good cause—more than one, in fact.

Stevie had been looking at entry slips for so long that she hadn't had a chance to look at the mural for a long time. She was astonished to see how much work had been done on it, and now that she wasn't selling tickets or counting them, she took a good long time to check it out.

Phyllis Devine was there, too.

"It's wonderful!" Stevie said, looking at the glorious collection of drawings. She found what she thought was a panda, next to a lopsided sugarplum fairy, not far from what looked like Superman trying to trap a navel orange—or maybe it was a pumpkin. She found a balloon hovering over three witches and a ghost. Next to them were none other than three blind mice and a farmer's wife. She thought she sensed the fine hand of Kate Devine there. She was pretty good with a paintbrush. She also saw Christine in her gleaming white outfit, including the cape. The cape made Stevie remember her ride and the one mysterious aspect of it. Where had John gotten the cape he'd worn?

And where was John in the mural? She was sure he would have wanted to leave his mark, but she searched every inch of the mural and couldn't find the headless horseman. Then, in a corner, up high in the sky, she found his mark. It wasn't the headless horseman at all. It was the silvery stallion, sleek and beautiful, with a nick in his ear. He had no rider in the picture. There was no cape, no young lovers—just the horse, proud, wild, and free.

Although Stevie thought John was a pretty odd young man, she had to admit that he sure did know how to ride a horse, and he sure knew how to draw one!

"THAT'S THE LAST bag of garbage," Carole announced proudly, putting the black plastic bag outside the back of the high school.

"Then that's the last bit of cleanup we have to do," Stevie said. The deal had been that if they ran the fair, disassembled the horror house, and took out the garbage, other volunteers would do all the rest of the cleanup. They were done. What they had come to the West to accomplish was complete. Finished. Successful.

"What do we do now?" Lisa asked, aware that she felt a little let down.

"Well, that's obvious, isn't it?" Stevie asked. "It's

Halloween night, we're in costumes, we go trick or treating!"

Only Stevie would think of collecting candy after an exhausting day of running the Halloween Fair. And that was just one of the reasons her friends loved her.

"So what are we waiting for?" Christine asked.

"Can John come with us?" Lisa asked. The girls looked at her curiously. "He worked very hard at the fair. He ought to have some fun, too," she said quickly.

Carole had the feeling there was more to it than that, but before she could ask, Kate answered the question. "I invited him, but he said he had to get back to the ranch. He wanted to check on the filly. I don't know why his father can't do that—"

Lisa knew. She almost spoke up, but that wouldn't have been fair to John. He'd told her the story of his sister's and his mother's death and the effect it had on his father when they were alone. He surely wouldn't want her to share the information with her friends.

"He just loves the filly," she said. "She's awfully cute, you know."

Stevie clicked her tongue to get Stewball moving, and then when everybody else was at a comfortable walk, she said, "I'm sure he does love the filly, but I wouldn't count on his going back to The Bar None.

He's probably waiting for us somewhere on the stallion in his white costume, ready to give us another show."

"What do you mean 'another show'?" Lisa asked.

"Well, you know how he followed us when we went to Christine's?" Kate said.

"It was pretty dark then," Lisa reminded her friends. "We don't know for sure that that was John on the stallion. We don't even know for sure that there was anybody on the stallion. There just *seemed* to be a rider on the horse's back."

"Let's try this house first," Kate said, interrupting the conversation. "The woman has worked for Mom at the ranch. They have lots of kids, and look at the pumpkin on their porch. I bet the candy's great!"

The girls rode up to the house and called "Trick or treat!" from their saddles.

The door soon opened. The three blind mice, the farmer's wife, and White Eagle all accepted the offer of homemade caramel apples—and moist paper towels so they could clean their hands right after they finished eating!

"You're the perfectly prepared Halloween host!" Kate said as thanks.

"Seems the least we can do for the group that made it possible to have an after-school program on the reservation. So thank *you* all. And have a good ride!"

The family waved a cheery good-bye and then closed the door.

"How did they know?" Stevie asked.

"It's a small town," Kate said. "Everybody knows everything."

"Everything?"

"Everything," Christine agreed.

The next house seemed to confirm the idea. The little girl who answered the door took one look at them and shrieked to her mother—"Mommy! It's the mouse who taught me how to ride a pony!"

Carole laughed. She barely recognized the child out of costume, but obviously the child remembered her, and she had the nice warm feeling that she'd started this little girl on a long and happy journey as a devoted horseback rider.

Her friends were happy about that, too, because the net result was measurable in their candy bags. The little girl's mother was *very* generous.

The house after that was the home of the panda who had won the dollhouse. It seemed that that child's parents couldn't say enough about how wonderful the party had been and how fabulous the dollhouse was. They knew the Lonetrees and gave Christine messages for her mother about what a great thing she'd done.

"Just wait until they see what it's like to have every-

body in the class come over every day after school!"
Stevie joked as they rode away. "It's going to be like a
feeding frenzy."

"Like we're going to have with all these goodies later
on?" Kate asked, patting her candy bag.

"Exactly the same," Stevie said. She was known for
her sweet tooth. She was even looking forward to the
inevitable stomachache.

Carole leaned forward and patted Berry on the
neck. Then she took a moment to look around at her
friends, decked out in Halloween costumes and riding
horseback.

"You know, I've been trick or treating in a lot of
different places. It's always been fun, but it's never
been like this. Do you have any idea what we look like,
walking our horses around Two Mile Creek, dressed up
the way we are?"

"Pretty silly, I'm sure, but it seems to be working,
doesn't it?" Kate answered. "Actually, I've had some
pretty unusual Halloweens. I remember one time I
went as a robot. I couldn't walk because I was wearing
all these big cardboard boxes. That was funny."

"Once I was a pirate," Stevie recalled. "I decided I
should have a wooden leg, so I folded one leg up in my
jeans."

"That must have been scary!" Lisa said.

"Sure was. My leg got so numb I couldn't walk for an

hour after I got home. The worst part was that my candy bag was in the other room and my brothers wouldn't bring it to me!"

The image of Stevie separated from her goodies by a numb leg got all five girls laughing.

"Well, all I can say is that there's never been another Halloween like this for me," Carole concluded. "And since it's highly unlikely that another Halloween will ever be this good, I think this will be my last year trick or treating. What a way to go out!"

"Definitely in glory," Stevie agreed. "And speaking of fabulous Halloweens, I haven't even had a chance yet to tell you all what happened to me when I was on the way to get the dollhouse at Christine's."

"Yeah, tell us!" Christine said. "Dad told me your horse showed up before you did. I forgot to ask what that was all about!"

"Well, settle back in the saddle, take a bite out of your caramel apple, and listen to my tale, because every word of it is true," Stevie said. Then she told them what happened—down to the tiniest, scariest detail.

"At first I was afraid," she began. She didn't mention that she was also scared at the middle and the end. For most of the adventure she'd been alone, and nobody was going to contradict her.

As her tale progressed, she elaborated elegantly

about the owl she'd seen. In the retelling his feathered wings had brushed her cheeks!

"Oooh!" Lisa said, frightened by the thought.

Then the branch that grabbed her hair had seemed to dig in and pull relentlessly. It wasn't exactly true, but it was more or less what Stevie had *thought* was happening at the time. Finally, when she got to the part about the coyote howling, Stewball bolting, and the rattlesnake threatening, she found that she didn't have to embellish at all. The entire story was simply terrifying.

"You mean you could hear him, but you had no idea where he was?" Christine asked.

"That's right. I was petrified. I did the only possible rational thing."

"You froze," Kate said, knowing that was the right thing to do.

"Well, that, but I also did something else. I screamed my head off."

"You did?" Christine said, horrified. That seemed like a very bad idea to her.

"Yes, and it's a good thing I did. Because John was there on the stallion. I guess he knew I'd gone out, and he was just waiting to make a mysterious appearance. But when I screamed, he came to my rescue."

She told them then how he'd swept by, lifted her off her feet onto the horse behind him, and had ridden her to the Lonetrees', dropping her off without a word.

"I was a little annoyed that he was still doing his phony Indian routine to try to convince us that the story was real, but I certainly wasn't annoyed that he was there to help me when I needed him the most."

"Wow," Kate said. "I'm impressed."

"How can you thank him!" Carole said.

"What a coincidence!" Kate said.

"No way," said Lisa.

"Huh?"

"No way," Lisa repeated.

"What do you mean 'no way'?" Stevie asked. "I'm here. I'm alive. I definitely got saved. It happened."

"Oh, I'm sure it happened," said Lisa. "Just the way you said. Except for one thing. It wasn't John."

"Of course it was," Stevie said. "Who else could it be? I mean, at first I even thought he was wearing Christine's cloak until I realized that I was wearing it. I don't know where he got his costume or when he changed, but he was definitely there."

"It's not possible," said Lisa. "I know where John Brightstar was all afternoon because he never left the horror house."

"Are you sure?" Stevie asked.

Lisa thought before she answered. She didn't want to tell her friends what she was feeling about John, and letting them know how carefully she had watched would reveal more than she wanted. Still, she was sure, and she could tell them that.

"I'm sure," she said. "Somebody saved Stevie out here this evening, but it wasn't John. I'm sure of that."

"Then who was it?" Stevie asked.

The question hung in the air. Five girls were wondering the same thing. Five girls considered the fact that it was Halloween, a night when strange things were supposed to happen.

14

"OKAY, PASS THE popcorn and I'll tell," Lisa said.

"Keep the popcorn from her and she'll tell faster," Stevie teased.

Carole wasn't sure what to do. The three of them were in her bedroom having their first Saddle Club meeting since returning from The Bar None a week ago, and Lisa seemed to be on the verge of telling her friends some very interesting news about a certain wrangler's son from the dude ranch.

"You mean you and John Brightstar . . . ?" Stevie asked.

Lisa blushed.

"That's enough of an answer for me," Carole said.

She handed the bowl to Lisa, who took a handful and then gave the bowl to Stevie.

"He's really nice," Lisa said.

"We know that," Stevie said. "Although he appears to me to be a bit mysterious. But the question is just *how* nice?"

"Really nice," Lisa confirmed.

"How did you get to be so friendly?" Carole asked. She just wanted to know how these things happened.

"I held the ladder for him an awful lot, as you'll recall," Lisa said.

"Is that what you were doing when I got you to help me look at the entry slips?" Stevie asked.

Lisa remembered the moment. How could she forget? "Yes, that's what we were doing. At first I was just holding the ladder, then I was, well, uh, kind of holding his hand."

"You were?"

"Yeah," Lisa said. "Until one of my best friends interrupted me."

It was Stevie's turn to blush. "I'm sorry," she said. "I had no idea."

"I didn't think you did," Lisa said. "Otherwise I would have wrung your neck—just the same as you would do to me."

"You bet I would," Stevie agreed. "Anyway, did you get to see him again before we left?"

"Yes," Lisa said. "I saw him in the barn on Sunday morning—you know, just to say good-bye. It was kind of nice."

Her friends knew what she meant. They didn't have to ask, and they were very happy for her.

There was a knock at the door. Colonel Hanson stuck his head in. "Letter for you today, honey," he said, handing an envelope to Carole. Carole took it and looked at it excitedly. "Oh, it's from Kate, and I bet she's writing to tell us what happened at the horse adoption!"

Carole tore open the envelope and began reading out loud.

*"You're hearing from the proud adoptive parent of a beautiful wild horse. She's a mare—mostly quarter horse, I think, and she's got a foal, too! They're both sorrel. I've named the mare Moon Glow. She's so beautiful I can't wait to show her to you girls. You've got to come back and meet her. Walter says we should start gentling her—that means getting her used to a halter and a lead rope—within a week or so. After that, we begin the real training. She's got wonderful lines. I know she's going to be a fine riding horse for me someday, and her foal is a beauty, too."*

"But what about the stallion?" Lisa asked. "What does she say about that?"

Carole continued reading.

*"I suppose you want to know about the stallion and, frankly, so do I. I can tell you what happened, but I certainly can't explain it.*

*Dad and I went to the adoption, looking for the stallion. We'd even spoken to the man in charge of it to warn him that was the horse we wanted. He said he didn't know the horse we meant, but since we'd had our application in for so long, we should have a good selection, as long as we got there early.*

*It was the stallion's herd all right. I recognized some of the mares. You would have, too. But there was no sign of the stallion. There was a stallion with the herd, but he wasn't silvery, and he didn't have a nick in his ear. In fact, he was a kind of ugly skewbald pinto.*

*Dad and I asked all the Bureau of Land Management people about the silvery stallion with the nick in his ear. Every single one of them said they'd never seen such a horse with this herd. Never seen a horse like that around here. So, what do you think?"*

"Oh, my," Lisa said, almost involuntarily. She could still see the stallion. She knew he existed. Didn't he?

"I don't understand," said Carole. "We actually *saw* that horse—more than once."

"There has to be an explanation," Stevie agreed. Then she turned to Lisa. "Look, you're the logical one here. What do you think is going on?"

"Maybe that skewbald just looks silvery white in the moonlight," Carole said. "We never did see him up close or in good light, you know."

"Maybe," Stevie said. "But I still think John's behind this."

"John was with me," Lisa reminded her friend.

"Then his father! It must have been Walter. It was just a big hoax."

"Maybe," Lisa said. In her heart, though, that wasn't what she thought. In her heart, she could see the spirit of White Eagle rising from the flames of the fire, joining the spirit of Moon Glow on the back of the white horse who had brought them together and who carried them to the skies to unite them for eternity. She could also imagine John as a young boy, hearing his mother tell him the tale, and loving the image of the free horse roaming the desert. "And maybe not," she said. "But you know, there's one thing that seems right, and that is that as much as I would have liked Kate to have the stallion, if she's not going to be the one to own him, nobody is. Somewhere out there—maybe on the plains or the desert, maybe even in our imaginations—the silvery stallion is roaming free and wild. He is there to help those who do good for the Native American people. That's the way it ought to be, you know."

At first Carole and Stevie didn't answer her. They were lost in their own thoughts—visions of the silvery stallion with the nick in his ear.

"Maybe," Stevie said, finally.

"Yeah," Carole agreed. "Maybe."

## About The Author

Bonnie Bryant is the author of nearly a hundred books for young readers, including novelisations of movie hits such as *Teenage Mutant Ninja Turtles*™ and *Honey, I Blew Up the Kids*, written under her married name, B. B. Hiller.

Ms Bryant began writing The Saddle Club in 1986. Although she had done some riding before that, she intensified her studies then and found herself learning right along with her characters Stevie, Carole, and Lisa. She claims that they are all much better riders than she is.

Ms Bryant was born and raised in New York City. She lives in Greenwich Village with her two sons.

464

# the Saddle Club

## Collect the series

BOX HILL HIGH SCHOOL
RESOURCE CENTRE

**COMING SOON**